Over the Edge

Vandana Kumari Jena is a retired officer of the Indian Administrative Service. She writes novels, short stories and poems. Her short stories have been published in over twenty anthologies. Her works include two novels—*The Dance of Death* (2008) and *Clueless* (2019); three collections of short stories—*The Incubation Chamber* (2014), *The Future is Mine* (2015) and *One Rotten Apple and Other Stories* (2018); and a collection of middles—*In the Middle* (2015). She lives in Mumbai.

Over the Edge

VANDANA KUMARI JENA

RUPA

Published by
Rupa Publications India Pvt. Ltd 2022
7/16, Ansari Road, Daryaganj
New Delhi 110002

Sales centres:
Allahabad Bengaluru Chennai
Hyderabad Jaipur Kathmandu
Kolkata Mumbai

Copyright © Vandana Kumari Jena 2022

All rights reserved.

No part of this publication may be reproduced, transmitted, or stored in a retrieval system, in any form or by any means, electronic, mechanical, photocopying, recording or otherwise, without the prior permission of the publisher.

This is a work of fiction. Names, characters, places and incidents are either the product of the author's imagination or are used fictitiously and any resemblance to any actual person, living or dead, events or locales is entirely coincidental.

ISBN: 978-93-5520157-7

First impression 2022

10 9 8 7 6 5 4 3 2 1

The moral right of the author has been asserted.

Printed at Thomson Press India Ltd., Faridabad

This book is sold subject to the condition that it shall not, by way of trade or otherwise, be lent, resold, hired out, or otherwise circulated, without the publisher's prior consent, in any form of binding or cover other than that in which it is published.

To my late husband Prasanna,
my sons Prakrit and Ankit and
my grandson Alexander, the light of my life.

Contents

1. Over the Edge — 1
2. A Storm is Brewing — 10
3. Surabhi — 20
4. Ghost Story — 31
5. Queen for a Day — 36
6. Burning Bright — 45
7. The Outsider — 53
8. Breaking Barriers — 61
9. Guilt — 68
10. Ring of Fire — 74
11. Nightmare — 84
12. Blood Wins — 92
13. Essence of a Woman — 98
14. Coma — 104
15. Hell Hath No Fury — 115
16. The Quest — 124

17. After the Storm	136
18. The Betrayal	144
19. Eureka Moments	153
20. The Ambush	161
21. Waverly	168
22. The Façade	186
23. The Gold Chain	196
24. The Iconoclast	204

Over the Edge

There is nothing I dislike more than the smell of jasmine joss sticks. I find it cloying. As the smell pervades the room, it brings back memories. I do not need memories today.

The pandit begins to chant the Gayatri mantra. We all chant after him. Repeating the mantra is believed to bring peace to the departed soul. This is a mantra we all know. Death is inevitable; it happens in every family.

Rahul's photo, garlanded with marigolds, has been placed atop a small table. We do not have a chowki in the house. We were not preparing for death. Rahul died at the age of thirty-seven. He does not need these rituals. He is at peace with himself. Or so I hope.

'Poor Manisha.' I catch a faint murmur behind me. *Mamta?* I do not know. 'She has a long and lonely life ahead of her.' Definitely Mamta; my cousin, my friend, my soulmate. *I must concentrate on the havan.* It is for Rahul's soul. This is not the time to play atheist. I lower my head in obeisance.

'Who knows what happened?' I hear another voice. A waspish, shrewish tone. Unmistakable; it's Nanda's. Rahul's sister. She is sheer poison. I would rather be friends with a rattlesnake. I can imagine the shocked expression suddenly colouring Mamta's face. I can visualize the slightly vacuous expression Mamta must have assumed; her mouth open, her lower lip protruding, her eyes bulging. Only I know it is a pose. One she assumes when she wants to play the simpleton. She actually has a razor-sharp mind. It is what makes her such a brilliant lawyer.

Panditji is too busy chanting the Gayatri mantra. He hears none of these murmurings. In any case, he is hard of hearing. He is blissfully unaware of the undercurrents.

Why am *I* surprised by Nanda's barb? I should have anticipated it. People are likely to gossip, and Nanda has an axe to grind. Someone lights another joss stick. I begin to feel nauseous. I am not allergic to joss sticks, just to jasmine. I shake my head. Memories begin to flood in. Rahul standing beside a jasmine shrub, waiting for me outside the college hostel, unabashedly inhaling the scent of the flowers. College romances are the best. They usually last the longest.

There was a time when I loved the smell of jasmine. It was not just a scent; it was the sweetest of emotions. I close my eyes. I recall Rahul bringing me vials of jasmine attar from Lucknow, which I would immediately dab on my wrists, to be surrounded by the fragrance. Other memories begin to seep in. Rahul bringing home a gajra of jasmine flowers and weaving it into my plaited hair, inhaling deeply, saying 'heavenly', before carrying me to the bedroom, my skin smelling of jasmine and his of musk, his favourite cologne. We would remain there all night, enveloped in a medley of heady perfumes. Those were such blissful days and not so long ago. After all, eight years is long, but it is not a lifetime.

'Concentrate,' I chide myself, *'Don't let your mind wander. Concentrate.'* But here, right now, the mind is the master and I am its slave.

'They were alone in Matheran', the waspish voice of Nanda intrudes, 'they were returning from Pune.' Her voice is no longer a whisper. This, I realize, is the beginning of the slander. A campaign started by Nanda. I am a marked woman.

My husband died in an attempt to take a selfie at Louisa Point, in Matheran. He slipped and fell into the deep, 900 feet valley below.

'It's certainly a dangerous place,' said Mamta. 'Don't you remember? A few years ago, a woman from Delhi slipped and fell from the same lookout point.'

'Yes,' said Nanda, 'but at that time, there were strong winds and a heavy fog. The weather was clear when Rahul died.'

Nanda must have looked up the case on the internet. No one could have remembered these details. The implications are clear. Nanda is accusing me. Nanda is accusing me of murder.

Mamta takes up the cudgels on my behalf. 'Nonsense,' she says robustly. 'Rahul's death was an accident. The police have also called it an accidental death. The injuries on his body are consistent with his fall.'

'Ha,' says Nanda. She doesn't need to say anything further. The scorn in her voice speaks volumes. 'The only one present there—apart from Rahul—was Manisha. Only she knows the truth.'

'Nonsense,' says Mamta again.

'Is it?' asks Nanda, in a not-so-soft whisper.

Who knew how it would end. I close my eyes, my mind far away. Far from the one thousand repetitions of the Gayatri mantra Panditji has decided to chant for Rahul.

It was a deliciously beautiful morning. The kind that brims with the smell of jacaranda wafting up to the balcony, that leaves one transfixed after watching the flight of parrots, when the wind lashes upon one's face, blowing tendrils of hair on to one's cheeks; when a loved one nestles close to you, whispering sweet nothings, just as one had thought that the age for romance was long past. But Rahul was nature's beloved, chiselled by the gods, groomed by its bounty and made for love.

I turned to look at him and was stunned by his sheer good looks all over again. His features seemed sculpted, his eyes were hooded and a faint smile played on his lips. He seemed like a child up to some mischief. I had never seen him so happy, not in recent years at least.

He ruffled my hair gently as I drove slowly down the road. I played the song '*Yeh moh moh ke dhaage*' on the stereo. How I love that song. And the lyrics, they seem to have been written just for us. Unwittingly, a tear rolled down my cheek; was it for my yesterdays or my today? I did not know.

'I want a cup of tea,' I said after a while, as the car cruised along the road. It was better than admitting that I needed a loo break.

'There are no fancy restaurants here,' said Rahul. He obviously knew the roads of Raigad a lot better than I did.

'Even a dhaba will do,' I said.

'No loo at a dhaba,' said Rahul astutely. I smiled. I had been caught. Rahul always had the uncanny knack of reading my mind.

We went to Olympian Heights, a dhaba, but disguised as a restaurant. The lone waiter served us two cups of chai. The tea was strong and sweet, served with large amounts of ginger. I ordered a plate of dal vada as well; the mountain air had made me feel famished. I broke a piece of the dal vada and munched on it. I was happy. I stole a glance at Rahul. How he had changed over the years. I had been admiring his chiselled face and debonair looks only a little while ago. How had I missed the frown lines on his forehead and around his mouth? Do we look at people and see what we wish to see and not what they really are? Now that I was looking at him carefully, I noticed how time had ravaged him. I raised my hand tentatively to remove the lock of hair that had fallen on his face. He jerked his face away. 'Don't,' he said, his tone even.

Rahul was right. There was no loo in Olympian Heights. *'Damn,'* I said to myself, *'I will have to find another dhaba soon.'* I paid the waiter and returned to the car. A little ahead, I saw a petrol pump. We did not need petrol. The fuel tank was almost full. But I had spotted the 'Suvidha' sign on a little shack near it. I shut the car door.

'Will you be all right?' I asked Rahul, hesitant.

'Of course, I will. What's wrong with me?' he asked.

The washroom was clean. *'Swachch Bharat is really at work,'* I noted wryly.

I drove along the ghat road, drawn to the green foliage stretching out in front of us. A squirrel with a long and bushy tail scurried past. Not a squirrel, I realized. Probably a fox. I cheered up. I love wildlife. I kept my eyes peeled. A little while later, I saw a flying squirrel, hanging spryly from a tree. After some time, we reached Matheran.

Rahul asked me to take a turn.

'Where are we going?' I asked, although I was the one driving.

'Louisa Point,' he said, 'it is a lookout point. You will love the view.'

I smiled indulgently at Rahul. He seemed animated. For

months he had been depressed. No, make that years. Ever since he had had the accident. I parked the car where the path narrowed, and we got off and began to climb towards the top.

'The view from there is spectacular,' he said, and he was right.

I breathed in deeply as I looked down into the valley. The mountain air was pure and refreshing. I felt like I could stay there forever.

'I have something to tell you.' I turned to Rahul.

'Just a minute,' Rahul said. 'I must capture this spectacular view.' He slowly stepped beyond the railing, phone angled to take a selfie. And then, his foot slipped. He fell headlong into the valley, his cries reverberating in the air.

I screamed. I rushed after him. I saw him as a tiny speck down below.

My blood ran cold. *No one could survive this fall.* I rang the police and then sat shivering in the car until the police arrived. They were very kind. The Sahyadri Rescue Team with a few local Adivasis left to search for Rahul's *body*. It was recovered after eight hours. The post-mortem was conducted at the local hospital. Rahul had multiple fractures—on his skull, his right femur and on his left arm.

His injuries were consistent with a fall, just as Mamta said. The police filed a report of accidental death. Rahul's body was released soon after. His nephew performed the last rites.

All through the havan, Nanda glares at me with venom. I realize just how far the venom had spread when a police inspector arrives soon after the havan. 'We have had a complaint regarding the cause of death,' he says, eyeing me shiftily while his eyes dart towards Nanda's face.

Mamta jumps to my defence. 'A post-mortem was done,' she

says belligerently. 'There was nothing suspicious about his death, was there? There were no bruises, no injury marks. Nothing to show he was pushed. He did not fall on his back, did he?'

The inspector looks sheepish. 'You are right,' he says. 'His injuries were consistent with a fall.'

Nanda clears her throat. 'Could she not have come up behind him and pushed him? Catching him unawares?'

Nanda probably hopes that after the police lockup and the third-degree interrogation, I will confess. There is a stunned silence across the room. Is that what happened? Only I know the truth. Everyone looks at me. I close my eyes.

'Let me tell you the truth, Inspector,' I finally say.

A look of triumph crosses Nanda's face. 'The truth shall prevail,' she mutters.

I begin my narration.

The story is the same one I had told the police earlier. It changes only when I get to Louisa Point.

'It seems like old times,' I had said at Louisa Point, injecting the right amount of enthusiasm into my voice as we turned towards the cliffside.

'The old times will never come back.' Rahul's voice was desultory. The apparent animation was now gone. Truculence had seeped into his tone. I looked at him questioningly. When we reached the top, we were entranced. The valley was beautiful. But Rahul first raised one foot over the railing, then the other. He stepped out to take a selfie, and then turned, and beckoned to me. I pointed to the warning sign. Rahul merely shrugged his shoulders, and I was forced to join him.

Suddenly, he turned towards me.

'So. You want me to go to this home, do you?' he asked, his

voice low. 'To deal with what you call my "persecution complex". I am a psycho, am I? You think my mind is unhinged?'

'No, Rahul, no,' I pleaded, surprised. 'After you ... ran over the boy in that car accident, you have been *traumatized*.'

'So, you think I killed him in cold blood?' he asked.

'No, no,' I said, 'it was an accident. You couldn't help it. He ran in front of the car. He carried a suicide note with him. He had a death wish.'

Rahul raised his hands to his face and began to weep. 'I hear voices in my head, Manisha,' he said. 'I am scared.'

'I know, I know,' I said soothingly.

'Rahul,' I said, a minute later, 'I have something to tell you.'

'I know,' he said, 'you are taking me to Dr Manchanda's Nursing Home, so that you can institutionalize me. The great Dr Manisha Tiwari, Head of the Department of Psychology.' There was a mocking note in his voice. He gripped my shoulders and dug his nails in.

'Stop it, Rahul, you are hurting me,' I shouted.

'What about the times *you* have hurt me?' he snarled, and I saw in his eyes the frustration I was so familiar with, which began when his start-up failed while my career zoomed, when he was unable to hold on to the jobs he took subsequently while I became busier at work, when he spent most of his time at home while I spent most of mine outside it. Suddenly, Rahul began to push me towards the edge of the cliff. His hold on me tightened. My shoulders hurt. I was petrified.

'No, Rahul—don't,' I said, my voice dry and hoarse. But he was relentless. I felt helpless in his grasp. But, in the end, the instinct of self-preservation gave me strength. I wrenched myself free from his grip, jumped over the railing and ran.

He tottered unsteadily on his feet, the recoil making him lose his balance. He slipped, and fell, careening down the cliff, his screams echoing all through the 900-foot fall.

'She has no proof,' Nanda says hotly, having heard my story.

'I do,' I say flatly.

For too long I have tried to protect Rahul. For too long I have tried to maintain the façade of a happy marriage. It is time for the truth, the whole truth and nothing but the truth.

I throw my pallu down and pull the blouse so it falls from my shoulder. Large ugly weals stand out on my skin, already turning bluish yellow. The inspector averts his eyes. But now, I am seething with anger. Next, I pull down the blouse from the other shoulder, revealing identical weals.

'I am willing to go with you for a medical examination, lest Nanda accuse me of self-inflicted injuries.'

Even Nanda looks horrified now.

'I hope you believe me now,' I say, my voice shrill. Mamta puts her hand on my wounded shoulder and I begin to weep. I do not know who the tears are for—myself, for Rahul, or for my unborn child, my baby who will never know his father.

A Storm is Brewing

A storm is brewing tonight. There have been many storms in my life but none like this one. This is a tangible storm. I can hear the wind lashing outside the window; the velocity must be very high. The windowpanes rattle loudly. I can hear a tree fall. I wonder which tree it is. Possibly a eucalyptus, which is not a very sturdy tree. The eucalyptus tree reminds me of human relationships. Some relationships are like the eucalyptus. They are not very sturdy either. I am like the eucalyptus.

I sit on an armchair beside Aparna, a thin Rajasthani quilt covering me, but I still shiver. We are neither in Bhubaneswar, nor is this cyclone Fani. The wind velocity is nowhere near 200 kmph or 150 kmph but it seems as if this house, with its very sturdy foundation, may still blow away. I can now hear the rain lash against the windows. I do not think the glass panes will be able to bear this onslaught for much longer. I am sure that if the windows break and the glass shatters, water will begin to flood in.

There have been many storms in both our lives, mine and my sister Aparna's life as well. I look over at Aparna sleeping peacefully, although she is usually fitful in her sleep. In her I try to see a reflection of myself, but fail. Aparna is everything I am not, although we are identical twins. Who would believe that we once shared an umbilical cord? We look alike, but that is the only thing we have in common. I am her antithesis—impulsive, impetuous and outspoken, while she is sensitive and caring.

Life has not been a bed of roses for either of us. We both have our crosses to bear. I have a son but no husband. I was widowed a year ago when I was just thirty-four. Aparna has a husband whom she loves dearly but no children. The irony of this is not lost on me. Aparna has had three miscarriages over the past twelve years and each time she has lost a child, she has lost a part of herself. I had a child without even trying to conceive.

Mohit is not back yet. I wonder what he finds so engrossing in the Physics laboratory. He has no sense of time when he is in his laboratory. Mohit works in the Indian Institute of Science, that venerable institute recognized today as the acme of scientific excellence—throughout the world. Aparna and Physics constitute his universe.

Bangalore is not known for its storms, at least these physical ones. But there are always exceptions. Climate change has already arrived.

Aparna is sleeping the sleep of the dead. I am happy to note this. Usually, she tosses and turns in her bed until Mohit returns home at night and holds her.

The rain abates a little. A while later, I hear Mohit's key turn in the lock. I then hear him walk into the bedroom. He sees me sitting by Aparna's bedside and his face softens somewhat. We have called a truce. We have begun to like each other. Perhaps 'like' is too strong a word. We have begun to *tolerate* each other.

'Do you want some dinner?' I ask him in a whisper.

'I am not very hungry,' he says, but I suspect it is only because he doesn't want me to play the surrogate wife. I shrug my shoulders. 'Suit yourself,' I am about to say and then I recall that we have called a truce.

Mohit has already left the room. I soon hear him in the kitchen. I hear crockery clang on the marble slab and the clatter of cutlery. Why can't he wake up the maid who is sleeping next to the kitchen, I wonder. With the noise he is making, he is going to wake Aparna. I rise from the bed and saunter into the kitchen.

'Here, let me heat up your food,' I offer. 'If you make too much noise, Aparna is bound to get up.' He looks at me like a chastened schoolboy who has been reprimanded by the headmaster. I quickly heat the rajma chawal, bhindi masala and paneer matar and hand it over to him on a plate. He sits at the dining table. I place a glass of water before him and draw out a chair for myself. I would like to talk to him but I don't want to intrude on his personal space, however it would be impolite to leave him alone.

It has been a month since I arrived in Bangalore. It is good that these are my son Mannan's summer vacations. But he sits glued to his iPad. I am not happy about it. I would be satisfied if Mannan were out climbing trees, playing football or running around the playfield to burn off the extra energy. Instead, he sits glum-faced in his room. Grown-ups bore him, especially his mother. I know because I was once like him. I was not like Aparna, who loved playing with dolls and teddy bears. I loved to climb trees—grazed knees and all—and to play kabaddi and run mini marathons. We may have been identical twins but we couldn't have been more different.

'How can you tell them apart?' Aparna's friend Smita had once asked Mohit, soon after they had gotten married. 'Aren't you afraid you will make a mistake, especially in the dark?' Smita likes to embarrass people. She has refined it to a fine art.

'Well,' Aparna had said sharply, 'Swapna does not live with us. And even if she did, she is not dumb, she can always shout!'

Mohit had added, 'A touch is all it would take for me to tell the difference.' I had squirmed at his implied criticism. I wondered why he was so disparaging of me. Was it because I did not conform to his image of the ideal woman? Perhaps I was this way because I knew that Papa had yearned for a boy. Instead, he had been blessed with two daughters. Maybe I had tried too hard to be the son I knew he was missing. Who knew. Maybe I was just wired differently. Maybe I did not want to be Aparna's clone. Since Aparna and I were identical twins, Ma told us that she would often feed me twice and wonder why Aparna was bawling so soon after she had been fed. Then Papa had come up with a solution. He had tied name tags on our hands and made us wear different coloured frocks so that no one would be confused. Still, teachers at school were often bewildered since we both were in our school uniform. I remember the time Aparna was punished in school for breaking a window, whereas I had been the culprit all along. Aparna had never forgiven me for not owning up.

It was not surprising that we both fell in love with the same man, but Mohit had eyes for no one but Aparna. I could not help falling in love with him, although I tried not to. Perhaps, I did not try hard enough. Love happens, as it happened to me, when Mohit's family moved into our neighbourhood. As it happened to Siddharth, Mohit's younger brother, who fell in love with me the moment he saw me. He proposed marriage to me every time we met, and I had always laughed it off. I knew that I could never reciprocate. How could I settle for second best when Mohit stood before my eyes? I loved everything about him, his brooding eyes, aquiline nose, his cleft chin and the unexpected smile that lit up his face. Unrequited love, it is said, is the best kind of love. It gives, without any hope of return. Mine, I knew, was destined to remain unrequited.

Mohit married Aparna as soon as he joined the Indian Institute of Science at Bangalore, after finishing his PhD in Physics from IIT Delhi. That was twelve years ago. Two years later, Aparna had her first miscarriage. I was in Delhi, but I flew down to Bangalore soon afterwards. Mohit was grateful that I was with Aparna to help her cope. Siddharth, who came to Bangalore a month and a half later, was delighted to find me still there.

When he proposed for the umpteenth time, I said yes. Siddharth was stunned. He had not expected it. We had a quiet wedding and returned to Delhi where Siddharth worked in an advertising firm. Seven and a half months later, I gave birth to Mannan, a healthy baby boy.

'It's a premature birth,' Siddharth informed Mohit. 'We're lucky that the mother and son are both fine.'

Mohit looked at me scornfully when he came to visit a few days later. 'He is 2.5 kg! That's the normal birth weight for a baby,' he said pointedly. He thought he understood why I had married Siddharth in haste.

'What are you implying?' I asked, my face bland.

'Nothing,' he muttered, looking away. But I knew what he thought. *'Trash'*—I think he labelled me that. I saw his eyes resting on Siddharth. Nobody could miss the look of pity in them.

Siddharth died eight years later while doing what he loved best, mountain climbing. Mannan performed the last rites. Mohit, who flew in when he got the news, looked at Mannan and was stunned. He saw Mannan's resemblance to Siddharth—the same curly hair, the aquiline nose, the almond eyes with sweeping lashes and the dimpled chin.

'I am sorry,' he said to me later. It was apology enough and I knew what he meant. But I was in no mood to forgive.

'What for?' I asked sharply. He blushed, unable to say anything more.

I have been with Aparna since she had her third miscarriage. A fortnight after my arrival, Aparna and Mohit called me to the drawing room. Aparna was unable to meet my eyes. I guessed there was a favour she wanted from me. A big one.

'The doctor says I have a problem with my uterus,' she said. 'I will not be able to bear another child. But I could have a child—with the help of a surrogate mother.' I kept quiet.

'Would you be willing?' she finally said.

I felt a sense of unreality creep over me. This couldn't be happening.

'You could be the surrogate, that way I would be able to monitor the baby's growth,' she said.

Aparna can be very convincing. She has always had me at her beck and call. When I needed her, however, right after Siddharth's death, she did not come. Of course, I do not blame her. She had just had her second miscarriage.

'*No!*' I shouted. 'I am a widow; don't you realize that?'

Aparna's face was blank. So wrapped up were Aparna and

Mohit in their own grief that they did not realize the implications of a widow becoming pregnant. I knew that Mohit had once thought of me as a slut. I did not want my son to think so too. Not now. Not ever. Or did they consider me such a non-conformist that public opinion would not matter to me? Or did Aparna hope that since we were identical twins, if the need arose, I could pass off as her?

'You could come and live with us,' coaxed Aparna.

I had guessed right. They had given the matter quite some thought. I was seeing a new side to Aparna. Did grief make one so selfish?

'What about Mannan and his school?' Mannan was not an inconvenience. He was my son. He was my entire life.

'You could shift him here,' she said.

'What about my job?' I asked.

It was obvious that neither Aparna nor Mohit thought much of my job as a teacher in a convent school. But I was emphatic in my refusal to be a surrogate. I told them to look elsewhere. A week later, Aparna and Mohit underwent some more tests and this time, when they returned, their faces looked even more tense.

'It has been ascertained that Aparna would need a donor egg ... as well as a surrogate mother,' said Mohit. I raised my eyebrows.

'Why don't you just adopt a baby? There are so many babies in this world who are in need of a loving home.' I said.

'But, Swapna, at least this way ... the baby would be Mohit's,' argued Aparna in a low voice. 'Why don't *you* donate?'

'The baby would be Mohit's and mine,' I argued. 'Is it not necessary to have an unknown donor?' I persisted.

'The doctor has promised to help,' Mohit said. I was surprised at the thought of what Aparna was suggesting.

'Why not take a donor egg from an unknown donor?' I suggested. Aparna argued that if I donated the child would look either like her or like Mohit. No one would guess the truth. Besides, the child would have no genetic diseases.

'I am sure they screen the donor for diseases,' I argued but I knew how it would work. I would be the unknown donor to donate her eggs to the fertility clinic. And by some fortuitous circumstance, my particular eggs would be picked for the IVF. 'There may be complications,' I said again.

'What complications?' asked Mohit. 'I know that you will not try to claim the child, even if it is biologically yours. It is not like we have feelings for each other.'

'I do not approve,' I said sharply. 'I do not think Siddharth would have either. I need time to think.'

I am lost in my thoughts as Mohit finishes his meal.

'So, what have you thought?' he says suddenly. I look up abruptly.

'About what?' I do not intend to make things easy for him. He hesitates. Then he says, 'You know what.'

'I am returning to Delhi in a week,' I say. 'Mannan's school starts then. And mine too.' I see his face pale. 'Siddharth made me very happy,' I add, 'but he did not leave me very rich.' Mohit's face turns red; I do not merely want to work, I need to work. And he knows this. Siddharth died young. We did not have much savings. And no insurance. I do not blame Siddharth. He did not expect to die at thirty-six.

'Aparna and I have been trying for a child for so long. Twelve years,' reminds Mohit. I can see the yearning in his eyes. Some people are obsessed with the idea of children. Having each other is never enough. Mohit and Aparna are like that.

'I want to be a father, Swapna,' he says, his voice pleading. I say nothing.

'You can make that happen,' he says and he walks out of the door.

'Why are you so blind, Mohit?' I scream silently. *'Can't you see?'*

But he doesn't see that the resemblances run in the family. Mannan looks like Siddharth—but he looks like Mohit too. Can't he see that? Did he never guess at why I married Siddharth in such a hurry? Did Mohit not remember that night at all? Did he never wonder? Or guess?

A storm had been brewing that night. A terrible storm. Aparna had been recovering from her first miscarriage. As the thunder rolled, she came into my room, as pale as a ghost.

'I am scared of the storm,' she said to me.

I held her in my arms and slowly rocked her to sleep. She slept in my room, lying half across my bed. There was no place for me to sleep, so I went to Aparna's bedroom and slept on her bed.

I have no recollection of when Mohit entered the room. He held me tight in his arms and smothered me with kisses, as he gently stroked my body.

I was numb with shock. Since Aparna had suffered a miscarriage, that they would make love was not a possibility I had contemplated. It must have been the first time after the miscarriage that he had decided to make love. There was something unreal about the whole thing. All my pent-up feelings erupted. This was what I had hoped for. I lay supine, as I suspect Aparna usually did—a passive partner. I inhaled his cologne and felt his arms tighten around me. I closed my eyes to stop the tears from falling. I felt fulfilled at last.

The next morning, Mohit left for work while I was still asleep in bed. I woke up, quickly left the bedroom and slept on the drawing room sofa. When Aparna woke up, she saw me curled up there.

I am sure that Mohit and Aparna never talked about that night. They had no reason to. And what could I have told Mohit? That I longed so much for my sister's husband that I did not tell him who I was, especially when I had all the time in the world to do so? A month later, I discovered that I was pregnant. When Siddharth proposed to me this time, I said yes. He rushed through the wedding before I had time to change my mind. I wonder why Mohit never suspected who Mannan's father was. Did he never look at Mannan and see his own reflection? I had no intention of telling Mohit the truth. I could not ruin so many lives. And I was afraid that if Aparna and he knew the truth they would take Mannan away from me.

Even after all these years, I hadn't stopped loving Mohit.

The storm that was brewing outside is getting louder. The rain that had abated somewhat when Mohit came in has now turned into a downpour. A storm is raging within me too. It has been ten years. Ten years is a long time. I still yearn for Mohit every night.

And every time a storm brews, I begin to hope.

Surabhi

It was not yet eight o'clock but I had already begun to get restless. The restlessness was increasing these days. It was understandable. Surabhi would be late yet again. She had to attend long meetings every Friday now. 'I'll be back by nine,' she had said, 'watch Netflix until then'; as though television were the solution to all my problems. I had watched everything on Netflix and Prime Video, and even Hotstar. Being housebound was not easy. Being ill was even more difficult. I was a bad patient, moody and irascible, although I was trying to change.

I was feeling stifled at home, even though the maid had left the windows wide open as she was leaving. I wanted to go out, get a breath of fresh air. I got up, locked the front door and went towards the lift. The power went off just then.

'Damn! Just my luck,' I cursed out loud.

I should have had a premonition that things were about to go awry. But I am not superstitious. I pride myself on being a rationalist. Anyway, there is a backup power generator in our housing society; the power was back within minutes.

Five minutes later, I walked out of our apartment complex, my head bowed, my pace slow and my kurta-pyjama hanging loosely over my thin frame. I had lost weight. I did not need a weighing machine to tell me that. I walked across the road to the new cafe that had opened only a week ago. I had seen the advertisement on a flyer that slipped out of the daily newspaper. It was not the coffee that I wanted. It was people I craved for.

Silence can be very unnerving at times. Voices on television can be jarring. Sometimes, just sometimes, one needs *someone* to talk to. I had Surabhi, but she would be back only after nine. I had an hour to kill.

Even from a distance I could see that the lights in the cafe were muted. *'To prevent customers from seeing the prices on the menu.'* I laughed cynically. The cafe seemed empty. But I was wrong. I noticed a couple sitting in the dim lights of the cafe when I walked in. I didn't know who they were until the woman turned and I saw that it was my wife.

I began to feel dizzy. Then I steadied myself. I was glad that she hadn't seen me. I went and found a table right at the back, where the lights seemed dimmer and I buried my face in the menu card. I hoped that Surabhi would not turn back and see me there. I could see the man with her. He was no one I knew, although I had a feeling that I had seen him somewhere before. He said something to her. From where I was sitting, I couldn't hear a thing. When I looked up, I saw him place his hand on hers. It was a curiously intimate gesture. It disabused me of any notion I had that this was an official meeting.

'One cappuccino, please,' I ordered.

The coffee arrived almost immediately. I sipped it slowly, trying to stall the gut-wrenching pain I was experiencing. '*Who was he? A colleague? An old client? A new neighbour? For how long had this been going on? Was she spending every Friday evening with him?*' I had a sudden urge to gulp fresh air, long gulps like someone starved of oxygen. I left my coffee unfinished, paid discreetly at the counter and left.

I returned to my apartment, my shoulders drooping. Twenty minutes later, the key to the door turned and Surabhi came inside.

'Why are you not resting?' she asked, seeing me sitting upright in the drawing room. I smiled. I was glad I could manage it. I had been practising it all this while.

'Where have you been?' I asked with just the right amount of indifference in my voice.

'Oh! I had to attend a meeting,' she murmured.

'Ah!' I said. There was the pregnant pause. 'Ah' meant nothing. Or it could mean something to someone who was looking for meanings. She slumped into a chair.

'God, I'm tired,' she said.

'Must've been a long meeting,' I murmured drily.

She looked at me searchingly. 'Yes,' she finally said.

After that, I began to keep a watch on her. There was nothing in her manner to arouse my suspicion. She was still the Surabhi I thought I knew. But now I knew better.

'Hey, wake up,' she said the next morning, ruffling my hair, 'it's almost eight o'clock.'

'I am not your sick pet poodle,' the words were on my lips, but I refrained from saying anything. I needed to be careful. I felt betrayed but I was in no mood for a confrontation.

Twelve years of marriage and what did I have to show for it? No children. Just a trophy wife. Someone stunning enough to stop you in your tracks. Someone who was midway on the corporate ladder. That is what I had wanted: a wife I could flaunt before friends. Well, here she was. I could not get the rancid taste out of my mouth. 'Jezebel,' I said silently to her back.

Surabhi returned from work that day, looking drained. Did she really have so much pressure at work, or was she torn between the two men in her life?

'Raghav, how are you?' she asked perfunctorily as she sank into the couch.

'I am good,' I said, my face devoid of emotion. After all, two can play at a game.

On Friday morning, she said, once again, that she would be late at work. 'Your boss is a workaholic,' I murmured.

'He is an absolute Tartar,' she said.

'Take your time, sweetheart,' I said cheerfully, 'work takes priority over everything else.'

At 8 p.m., I left home and walked into the cafe again. They were sitting at the same table they had chosen before. It must have been their favourite. We had had our favourite table too, Surabhi and I, but that was a long time ago. I chose the table right behind them. I wore a cap, although it was an ineffectual disguise, on the off chance that one of them turned around or walked my way. I need not have worried. They were totally absorbed in each other.

Their faces were in shadow. Although I had my back to them, I could still hear them speak. This time, I had chosen this table because I wanted to eavesdrop.

'So, what have you thought of my proposal?' she asked.

'I agree,' he said.

It was Surabhi who was proposing to him. Somehow, that did not come as a surprise. That was her style. Even when we were dating, while I dithered during our courtship days, it is she who had proposed marriage. *'What does she see in this tall man with a craggy face?* I wondered dispassionately. Whatever it was, it was clear that she had given up on me.

'You are a remarkable woman,' he said warmly, 'that is why I admire you so much.'

She was silent.

'Have you told him yet?' he persisted. He seemed very ardent in his pursuit.

She appeared to hesitate. 'Not yet,' she said softly.

'But you have to tell him sometime,' he insisted. She did not say anything. 'Tell me if you want to change your mind,' he said. 'I don't want you to have any regrets.'

'I have none,' she said. 'In any case, he has very little time left.'

I tried, but I couldn't stop my tears from rolling down in the dim light of the cafe. It was bad enough to know that I was dying. I now realized that my wife was simply waiting for me to die. The coffee I had ordered scorched my tongue. I gulped it down, the golden liquid burning my throat. Then I got up. With my shoulders slouched and my head bowed. I trudged back to our apartment. Surabhi came back fifteen minutes later, looking drained as usual. I would have thought that a meeting with her paramour would have rejuvenated her.

'Another long meeting?' I chuckled.

'Yes,' she said, yawning loudly, 'it was exhausting.'

How glib had she become. The falsehoods glided so smoothly off her tongue.

She had not always been like this. She had been different. She had been loving, compassionate and caring. It had been love at first sight for me, that trite phrase, which means nothing until it actually happens. Suddenly, all the mushy, meaningless phrases in romantic novels began to ring true for me. What did she ever see in me, a forty-year-old entrepreneur, twelve years her senior, I did not know.

'You're too modest,' she had said. 'You are an engineer from IIT Delhi and an MBA to boot.' Surabhi had brought me luck. My start-up took off and the business and profits had started to roll in. Who would have thought that providing pure milk at doorsteps could turn profitable? 'It was a felt need you addressed,' she enthused. 'It was a gamble which paid off,' I said modestly. I expanded my business and started a unit to supply fresh meat and poultry to customers. That succeeded as well. She said, 'You're a genius, Raghav, you really are. You think out of the box.' I had said indulgently, 'You are my lucky mascot.'

After our marriage, I began to believe in eternal bliss. That is, until ten years later, when my diabetes went out of control and I developed spiralling hypertension and chronic kidney disease. It may have been the work, that which invigorated me had also been taking a toll on my health and stress had aggravated all the underlying issues. I learnt that some day, I would need a kidney transplant. The diagnosis depressed me.

'There are disadvantages to being an only child,' I said morosely. 'I have no siblings who can donate their kidney.'

'Should I get screened?' she had asked.

'No, never.' I was horrified by the very thought. 'You are young, just thirty-eight.' I felt overwhelmed by the fact that she had even offered. But she persisted. I gave in to her demands reluctantly. But our blood groups did not match. I wonder which one of us was more relieved, she or I.

I was put on the waiting list to avail a kidney. Thus, the wait for a donor began. It would be a very long wait, I knew. Most kidney patients die without getting a transplant. A year later, when my condition deteriorated, I began to undergo dialysis. Life began to swing quickly between dialysis and work, dialysis and hope, dialysis and despair. With the passage of time, I became increasingly depressed and began to work from home. Thankfully, my businesses were well established. But sometimes I wondered if I should have known that my hold on life was tenuous the very day I was diagnosed. But one lives on hope. I wanted to live. There was so much I wanted to do. I was just fifty-two.

But now, I realized that Surabhi had already given up on me. She had found someone else. The woman who had once held *my* hand was now holding someone else's. I felt betrayed. I seethed. I raved. I ranted. But in private. We were marvelous actors, both of us. I would not let her pity me, neither would I confront her. I wanted to live out my last days in peace.

I received a phone call from the hospital one day.

'We have a possible donor for you,' the doctor said.

'A cadaver?' I asked.

'A live donor.'

'How is that possible?' I wondered out loud. Altruistic donors were often found abroad, but in India? I was asked to meet him. We met at the hospital. He introduced himself as Ravi Kumar. He was a young man, plain-looking and simply dressed. A number of tests were conducted, the blood and tissue typing, kidney function tests, etc. We met once again after the results came in and he proved to be a match.

'I am so grateful to you,' I said.

'I am too,' he said, 'especially to Surabhi madam.'

Then I understood. Surabhi had managed to find someone

desperate and willing enough to sell his kidney—in the garb of kidney donation. The hospital authorities must have decided to look the other way, because under the Transplantation of Human Organ Amendment Act, 2011, selling of organs was banned. I wonder how Surabhi had managed it. How much was Surabhi willing to pay for the kidney? One lakh? Five lakh? Ten lakh? Was this her grand gesture before she said goodbye? I should have felt angry, but I didn't; I was so grateful for the promise of a new lease of life. I was no longer clutching at straws. I had been thrown a lifeline. Surabhi, however, remained edgy and tense. I knew the reason. But the game of pretence continued.

I did not hear from the hospital for some time. I was afraid that my donor had backed out. Then suddenly, I got a call from the hospital, asking me to check myself in.

'The Authorization Committee had not given its approval till now,' Dr Shashank Raizada, my nephrologist, told me. 'Bureaucratic red tape,' he muttered. I nodded.

Surabhi took me to the hospital, her manner distracted and her face pale. The surgery was scheduled for four days later.

'I have to go to Thailand for business negotiations,' she told me firmly that evening. 'I will leave tomorrow morning.'

I was stunned. What could be more important than her husband's kidney transplant?

'It was planned a long time ago,' she said, not meeting my eyes. 'I will try to return in time for your surgery. Meanwhile, my cousin, Shashwat, will be with you.' This must have been a rendezvous they had already planned, I realized, but the timing had gone awry. Why couldn't she tell the man with the craggy face to postpone? I figured that the flight tickets and the hotel rooms must have been booked in advance.

Dr Shashank Raizada, my nephrologist, and Dr Pradeep Nayak, the urologist, entered my room just then. She could not meet their eyes as she left the room. The whole hospital must be pitying me, I thought, although no one said a word.

For two days, Shashwat was by my side, while I went through a number of procedures. I signed a flurry of papers without reading a word on them. Consent forms, insurance forms, God alone knows how many forms. I was sedated the night before the operation to keep me calm. When I woke up the next morning, Shashwat was lounging, half-asleep in the armchair. Surabhi had still not returned.

The nurses readied me for the procedure and I was wheeled into the operation theatre. *'I would have to learn to live alone,'* I realized suddenly, *'if I was lucky to come out of surgery alive.'* The operation lasted five hours. I was wheeled into the ICU six hours later. I had been warned about the dangers of infection, the need for immunosuppressants to prevent rejection and the need for frequent check-ups.

I was groggy when I came out of the anaesthesia. I wavered between wakefulness and drowsiness. When the effects of the anaesthesia wore off completely, I realized that Surabhi had not come to see me in the ICU. She was still in Thailand. Perhaps she did not plan to return at all. Ex-parte divorces were also granted, I knew. Then, he walked in, the tall man with a craggy face. He was wearing a white coat. Somehow, that fact did not register immediately. Why was he here? If he was here, where was Surabhi? He smiled at me and when he did, his whole face lit up. I realized why Surabhi had fallen for him. But I could not forgive him.

'Where is Surabhi?' I asked, my tone brusque, 'why isn't she here?'

He raised his eyebrows.

'You know why she can't be here, she's in a private room in the ward—' he began and then he stopped abruptly. 'You don't know? She never told you? How is that possible? She had promised she would,' he said quickly.

'Told me what?'

'That it is she who donated her kidney for you.'

'She didn't donate anything,' I said querulously, 'she is not a match. Ravi Kumar did.'

'That's true,' he said, 'it's a swap. Surabhi donated her kidney to Ravi Kumar's wife, he, in turn, donated his kidney to you.'

A long silence ensued.

'I am Dr Rajesh Kamath,' he filled in. 'I am a nephrologist on the donor team. That is why you have never seen me. For the past few months, Surabhi has been undergoing a battery of tests—psycho-social evaluation, as well as her own kidney function tests, blood and tissue typing test, etc. as a donor to that patient, Mr Kumar's wife. I met Surabhi a number of times, to counsel her about kidney donation and all that it entails. After all, it is a major decision and a risk. But Surabhi is doing fine.'

I was speechless. I remembered all the papers I had signed without reading. Maybe the consent for the swap was somewhere among them.

'I could not discuss the swap openly with you, nor could Dr Raizada or Dr Nayak,' continued Dr Kamath, 'because Surabhi was reluctant to tell you about it. She was afraid that you would refuse the swap. But she said she couldn't let you die. She said she couldn't imagine a life without you.'

'You are a very lucky man,' he added as he placed his hand on mine. He saw a series of expressions transfigure my face—disbelief, dismay, shock and regret. I now realized why Ravi Kumar was grateful to her and why none of the doctors were surprised by Surabhi's absence. They all knew.

Only I had not been told.

How I had misunderstood Surabhi! My tears began to fall and continued to fall.

Ghost Story

I love the dawn. As I see the golden glow of the morning sun filter through my window, I feel almost euphoric. On a sudden mad impulse, I get up and decide to go for a walk. I gaze tenderly at Sushant on the bed. He is not at peace with himself. He looks tired; his brows are furrowed, as though he is carrying a huge burden on his shoulders. I leave a kiss on his shoulder. He will not wake till I return. He sleeps like a log, although these days I have watched him toss and turn in his sleep.

I slip out quietly from the apartment, closing the door gently behind me. It has an automatic lock, thank god for that. I look speculatively towards the four lifts near our apartment and then suddenly decide to take the stairs. One would be crazy to walk down six floors when there are four lifts on my floor. But I like it, it will provide the necessary exercise and keep me lithe. I turn and look at my apartment. 6004. It is my lucky number. It adds up to 10, which happens to be my birthday. I do not really believe in numerology. It doesn't work, I know.

I begin my walk once outside the building. I love the breeze that blows across my face. I love Mumbai, although I am a Delhi girl. Mumbai is far less polluted than Delhi is. In Delhi, one needs to wear a mask to go for a morning walk. I do not know what is to blame—vehicular pollution or stubble burning in Haryana. In Mumbai, I can breathe in the fresh air. I take big gulps, enjoying the breeze.

I love the sea. I love the way the waves lash on the shore. I love the white froth on the foam. I wish I could capture it all on my camera. I love photos. I love selfies. It is a pity we do not live near the sea. We might as well be in Delhi, Gurugram or in Noida. But one's house has to be near one's workplace. It is a pity Sushant works in Vikhroli.

I turn around for a glance. I walk slowly, savouring the cool breeze. The water ripples in the swimming pool. I hear the train whistle past; the Ghatkopar railway station is close by. The central line runs right behind our society complex. I take a long walk, enjoying the morning air. The clubhouse is on my left. A few enthusiasts are already inside the gym. I can see them through the window. I have been in the gym with Sushant. There is a row of treadmills, exercycles and rowing machines for our use. People walk furiously on the treadmills. I wonder if it is the kilos that they want to lose, or whether they are trying to release their pent-up anger.

There is no one at the swimming pool. Perhaps it is too early to swim. I see a man on the exercycle, peddling furiously, opposite our apartment block. I walk slowly, taking measured steps, walking by the indoor pool in another building, climbing up the steps, towards the municipal garden. The garden is my favourite spot because it is usually empty. It is not that I dislike people; it is simply that I prefer solitude. Today, however, I see people. What a surprise. I bend my head a little to get through the gate.

There is a green and worn walker's path weaving through the garden which I usually take. I am surprised to see an old man with a pointy cap on his head. He has a flowing goatee. It is grey. I stare, astonished. His face doesn't look old. Some people grey prematurely, I surmise. He is sitting on the swing, looking contemplative. A burqa-clad woman is sitting quietly on a nearby bench. Next to her is a woman on an exercycle. She moves as though in slow motion. There is something surreal about this scene. I see a man walking on the pathway, his steps measured. I smile at the man on the swing. He looks through me. I am hurt. Never mind, I tell myself. Maybe he is uncomfortable greeting a woman, I try again. I nod pleasantly at the lady in the burqa and at the woman on the exercycle. Nobody acknowledges my greeting. I am shocked. *'Are they just rude or are they just not aware of social niceties?'* I brood as I walk past the canopy of trees. I am glad others cannot see me. The hurt rankles.

A little ahead, I see an elevated mound. It has been painted a vibrant blue. On its side are carved peacocks, their plumage painted in vivid colours. I am amazed by the artistry of the unknown painter. Further ahead, I see a small mound which encases a peepul tree. I shiver a little. I remember the rumours about the peepul tree. A thought just strikes me—maybe these people are not real. Maybe they are ghosts of people long dead. I remember that there is a graveyard quite close to our complex. Maybe the dead have been disturbed and have come here to take respite. Maybe they think that the deserted park belongs to them. Maybe they died not so long ago.

As I turn down the bending path, I see a poster of a film at a distance. It advertises the film *Hotel Mumbai*. I have seen it in the cinema hall. I went with Sushant. It was so poignant to watch the people trapped in Taj Mahal Hotel during the Mumbai attacks on 26 November 2008. Suddenly, I remember. Today is 26/11. Maybe these people were among those who were killed in the attacks. Maybe they were in the Taj Mahal Hotel, celebrating a birthday, when the attacks occurred. I remember watching a poignant short film about it as well, *Biryani* it was called. It took me a long time to figure out what happened in the end. I like movies like that.

Or maybe, these people were killed in the attacks at the railway station, which also occurred on the same day. Why did I not think about the Mumbai attacks on 26 November where so many people died.

Maybe this is a coincidence, maybe they died somewhere else. In a road accident, perhaps. Death always comes as an end, to everyone. To some it comes unexpectedly. It is often undeserved. The woman who fell in Bandstand and died while taking a selfie did not deserve to die, neither did the woman who died in our apartment building, when she leaned out of the balcony and the railing fell off. She fell down six floors, her head smashing as she hit the concrete. Her husband was devastated. Thank goodness they had no children. But how could they have? They had only been married for six months. The police had been suspicious about her death, but fortunately for her husband, the railing on the adjoining balcony broke soon after, and it became clear that shoddy construction was to blame and there was no mala fide intent on the husband's part. Who knows if her ghost still wanders.

I quicken my pace. I try to put all these thoughts out of my mind. I laugh at my overwrought imagination. Ghosts, indeed! Whatever will I think of next. These people may just be reserved. Or shy. I must return home. Sushant must be about to wake up, his brow still furrowed, his face still tense. He will make himself a cup of coffee and move towards the balcony and then stop. He has stopped going there ever since the railing in our balcony fell, which was two months ago, although it has since been replaced by a new one. He thinks it is an omen.

'Who are the people in the garden?' I asked the old chowkidar at the gate, my curiosity still unassuaged.

'Can you see them?' he asks, amazed.

'Why?' I ask.

'Only the dead can,' he whispers, suddenly afraid.

I look at him conspiratorially and wink. And then, I disappear.

Queen for a Day

There comes a moment in everyone's life when everything changes. She knew in her heart that this was hers. She woke up with a sense of well-being. She wanted to twirl on her toes, to jump down the stairs two at a time, to turn cartwheels across the corridor, to run around the garden. Kriti smiled wryly. She had let her imagination take wings. Where was the corridor? Where was the garden?

She rose gingerly from her bed, rolled the bedroll and placed it neatly in a corner and began dusting her tiny one-roomed quarter. Today was her twenty-first birthday. Something good was bound to come today. She could feel it in her bones.

She grimaced. She felt the same way every birthday. But this birthday would be like the last one and the one before it. She would go to the airport, insert her biometric fingerprint, collect her badge, walk towards the toilets and enter them with the usual sense of despondency. She would begin by cleaning the washbasins. She would ensure that the liquid soap was full in each dispenser, check that the toilet rolls were in their holders, mop up the floors after putting the 'Caution-Wet Floor' sign on the floor, and curse god for making her a Dalit.

'There is no shame in cleaning toilets,' her mother had said. 'You don't have to carry headloads of shit.' Kriti had squirmed. What about her own aspirations? she thought. She blamed her father for dying early. He had needed to live so that she too could live. But he had been hit by a car while crossing the road, becoming yet another statistic in the list of pedestrian deaths. 'What a waste,' she muttered under her breath. He should have lived, at least until she was able to lead her own life. 'This is only temporary, this job is only temporary,' she said to herself every day, afraid that it was just a matter of time before she would accept it as her only destiny.

She dressed with care, wearing the blue and purple salwar kameez her mother had bought for her. She loved the print and the satin-soft fabric in which she had buried her face when her mother had gifted it to her. Her mother placed a 1,000-rupee note in her hand.

'Janam din mubarak ho,' she said.

'Ma must really have saved for my birthday,' Kriti thought. It was a lot of money. On a sudden whim, she took out the same amount from her own savings and put it into her purse. She felt rich and on top of the world.

Once Kriti was inside the airport, she looked covetously at the shops inside. The Haldiram's shop, with the sweetmeats on display. The sweets did not interest her, but the dahi-bhalla and papri chaat did. She eyed the WHSmith shop, with its racks of books on display. She wanted to touch the books with their glitzy covers, as well as the Lavie handbags, which hung from the racks in a kiosk nearby. She looked at the Coffee Bean and Tea Leaf shop before her and wondered if the brownies tasted as scrumptious as they looked.

Then, she turned left and moved towards her assigned bathroom.

'Namaste,' she greeted the first passenger who rushed into the bathroom. The woman ignored her. Kriti was used to being ignored. It came with the territory. She was a nobody. Only, she didn't feel that she should be treated like one. Something told her she was special.

She was carefully placing the seat cover on the toilet seat when she heard a commotion outside the ladies toilet. A woman had fallen down, just outside the toilet. She was in labour, screaming in pain. A motley group of people had gathered around her.

'Quick, call for an ambulance, she needs hospitalization. She is in labour,' shouted someone. As the people bent down and lifted the woman, something flew towards Kriti. She looked at it. It was a boarding pass.

Her heart began to beat faster.

'Savita Tai, look at what I have got,' Kriti said, her voice giddy with excitement.

'No,' said Savita Tai, 'a big no.'

'I haven't said anything yet,' Kriti said truculently.

'I know what you're thinking, but no,' said Savita Tai. Kriti looked belligerently at her. 'Don't blame me if you get caught,' warned Savita Tai.

'How?' she shot back.

'You will go to jail,' Savita Tai threatened, not able to answer Kriti's query, 'and you will lose your job.' But Kriti was beyond reason. She rushed away. Ten minutes later, she returned, having discarded her uniform. She was wearing her blue and purple salwar kameez. Her hair, tied up in a tight bun earlier, was left loose. A big, maroon bindi adorned her face. She was a far cry from the uniformed sweeper in blue, wiping the toilet floor.

Just how many times had she seen people stride along on the travellator? Had she known that one day she too would travel on it, and emerge to stand in front of one of the gates? Kriti moved jauntily towards Gate Number 38. There was a long queue at the gate. She stood nonchalantly in the queue, trying to force her heart to not beat so loudly. *'Courage, girl,'* she told herself, *'Have courage.'* When the boarding was announced, she walked confidently to have the boarding pass checked and then entered the aircraft. The air hostess smiled at her and directed her towards her seat.

'It is a window seat!' she muttered in half-concealed excitement, feeling as though she was a seasoned traveller. A man came and sat next to her. She looked at him appraisingly and felt a little disappointed. He was years older than her. *'Must be forty,'* she surmised. Why had she expected a Varun Dhawan lookalike to sit next to her? The aircraft started to taxi. A sudden noise from the aircraft startled her. She winced.

'Your first time?' asked her neighbour, but his voice was kind, not condescending.

'So, what takes you to Jaipur?' he asked her as the flight took off.

'Inquisitive,' she thought, or maybe he was just trying to be polite. 'Adventure,' she said.

'Ah!' he said. 'If adventure is what you are looking for, you are going to the right place.' For a moment, she thought of the woman whose place she had taken. *'I hope she is all right,'* she thought to herself. She wondered idly whether the woman had a boy or a girl. Or was she still in labour?

'So, are you visiting your relatives in Jaipur?' asked her neighbour.

'Why does he ask so many questions?' she wondered resentfully, *'definitely inquisitive.'*

'No,' she said, answering in monosyllables. She then turned away and began to look out of the window.

The air hostess soon announced that the flight was about to land. Kriti was disappointed. It had been such a short flight. As the plane landed smoothly on the tarmac people started getting out of their seats. She was glad that she had given in to her whim to take a free flight. The flight had been all that she had wanted that day. She could now die happy. But suddenly, the enormity of what she had done, struck her. Her lips began trembling. As she trudged slowly to the arrival lounge, she began to sob.

Her co-passenger, who was walking beside her, was alarmed.

'Here, here, don't cry,' he said, not knowing how to pacify her. 'Tell me,' he said at last and she broke down. She decided to confide in him.

'Come,' he said, not knowing what else to say, as he took her to a cafe, 'you must be hungry.' Sitting at a table, slowly, haltingly, she narrated the entire story. He looked intently at her. Seeing this beautiful girl before him, he could not imagine her scrubbing floors and changing toilet seat covers. For a minute, he was repulsed, and then, as he saw the tears rolling down her face, he felt waves of sympathy wash over him, although all he said was, 'Happy birthday.'

On hearing his calm voice, she began to bawl. People in the cafe turned to look at him. 'Hush,' he said, 'don't cry or people will misunderstand.'

'What is it now?' he said, seeing the tears still rolling down her face.

'How will I return?' she said, sniffing loudly.

'You can always take a flight back,' he said.

'I have only ₹2,000 with me,' she said, 'which is not enough for a return ticket.'

'Let me buy you one,' he said, 'consider it your birthday present.'

She looked at him suspiciously. Why would he spend so much money on her? Did he expect to be paid for his generosity? She felt cynical. She knew all about the payment men expected from women. But she was not about to give in. She would shout. He did not seem the sort, but no one was altruistic without reason. Then he smiled.

'Don't worry,' he said, 'there are no strings attached.' Within minutes, her return flight was booked.

'Let me be your guide for the day,' he said, 'what would you like to visit in Jaipur?'

'How can you take me around? Don't you have work to attend to?' she asked curiously.

He laughed. 'I can afford to take a day off,' he said. 'I run my own business.'

'I know nothing about Jaipur,' she confessed, relaxing a little.

'How about the Jantar Mantar and the Palace?' he said.

She nodded.

They took a car to Jantar Mantar. 'I have seen the Jantar Mantar in Delhi,' she said when they entered, 'but this one seems bigger.' She listened to him, fascinated, as he explained that the Jantar Mantar was built by Sawai Jai Singh I, the founder of Jaipur.

'... the monument was completed in 1734. The sundial in Jantar Mantar is the largest stone sundial in the world and there are nineteen instruments in all in the Jantar Mantar.' Kriti was awed by the large structure and touched by the respect he showed her despite their differences.

'Now, I shall take you to the Palace,' said her escort. The Palace was not intimidating, at least from the outside. Her escort was a wonderful guide. She was spellbound as he told her about the City Palace, which was built by Maharaja Sawai Jai Singh II. She was overawed when she saw the two silver kalash, in which Maharaja Sawai Madho Singh II had carried water for himself during his stay in London. She was speechless when she saw the sileh khana with its huge collection of guns and ammunition. She was captivated by the paintings adorning the walls in the painting and photography gallery.

'Have you been to Johri Bazaar?' he asked her as they came out of the Palace.

Soon, they were standing outside a small shop, vying with other buyers in Johri Bazaar. She tried out several necklaces while he moved here and there restlessly, ambling along from shop to shop, while she was glued to the one selling costume jewellery. It was clear that shopping of this kind left him bored. At last, she bought a lacquer-work necklace in aquamarine. Then he said, 'It is time for you to return, birthday girl, or you will miss your flight, I shall take you back to the airport.'

He did not admit it to himself, but he had not had as much fun in years. He felt as though he was Gregory Peck and she Audrey Hepburn from the movie *Roman Holiday*. Except that Kriti was no princess. But that did not take away from the thrill of the day's adventure. Ever since his wife, Prerna, had died, he had become taciturn and morose. Today, after many years, he felt alive.

Kriti experienced a strange sense of regret as the taxi whizzed past the city and towards the airport. She wondered if she would visit Jaipur ever again, or if she would meet this man, who had been like her guardian angel. Once they got out of the taxi, they stood facing each other awkwardly, not knowing what to say.

'Have a safe flight,' he muttered at last. He had a strong urge to kiss her on her forehead, but he resisted such a paternal urge. She might misunderstand.

She looked at him. How she had misunderstood him! She wished that he would at least shake hands. This would be the last time that she saw him. This day would remain engraved in her memory forever. Just as she was leaving, he shoved his business card into her hand. 'In case you ever need to get in touch,' he said. Along with it was a small package.

'You already gave me my birthday present,' she reminded him in haste.

'This is a parting gift.' He smiled.

She smiled in return as she clutched it tightly in her hand.

This time, Kriti boarded her flight without fear and smiled as she saw her name on the boarding pass. She smiled at her co-passenger as she slipped into her seat, saw that he was at least sixty years old, and chuckled to herself. She opened the package curiously, wondering what her benefactor had gifted her, and laughed when she saw the present. Half an hour later, she stepped out of the plane and came out of Terminal 1D, at the Indira Gandhi International Airport. She started walking towards the bus stop. From a distance, she saw Savita Tai coming out of the airport from the Departure Terminal. She looked relaxed.

'I told Madan,' began Savita Tai, referring to their supervisor, 'that you were unwell, and were in such a rush that you forgot to sign out. Kriti, now don't return to work for at least two days.'

Kriti smiled at her, her humour restored, last worry assuaged. The young are resilient and so was she. She had flown on a plane. It had been a life-changing moment for her. It meant something. It meant that she was not meant to clean toilets all her life. She pulled her hair out of the hair-tie, combed it vigorously with her hairbrush, opened her parting gift, smeared the red lipstick on her lips and hailed a passing taxi.

Burning Bright

'It was a pleasure to burn the Ravana,' Nishant says.

'You mean the effigy!' I exclaim.

'The effigy,' he corrects himself.

'It was a pleasure to burn my tongue, sipping Starbucks' sizzling Macchiato.' I grimace.

He smiles. No one would recognize us when we sit like this with our white coats off. We look years younger—Nishant the surgeon and I, the anaesthetist. He chuckles. His eyes look unseeingly into the distance. The euphoria of yesterday has not yet disappeared. After all, not everyone gets the chance to play God. Perhaps the accolades are still ringing in his ears. Of course, we live in a small town, just a hundred kilometres from Delhi, and Nishant was chosen to play Rama because of his stunning good looks and his skill in archery. He had to strike down and burn the effigy with his bow and arrow. Clad in saffron robes, bow and arrow in hand, he had looked magnificent.

In Delhi, they would have had called for a professional artist and not had an amateur play the role.

'The victory of good over evil,' he says, alluding to the legend in which Lord Rama had killed Ravana, the king of Sri Lanka, for abducting his wife Sita and holding her hostage for a year. The day was celebrated throughout the country as Dussehra. Of course, no one really knows whether the legend was true or simply allegorical.

'You are very self-righteous,' I say lightly.

He bridles in indignation. He has caught the sarcasm in my tone. 'I am righteous, not self-righteous,' he says.

'You must learn to take a joke,' I say smoothing things. 'You must learn to let your hair down. Otherwise, you may end up single.'

I do not know him well enough to say anything more. I have seen him around for a few months.

'I had a wife,' he says.

'Had?' I raise my eyebrows.

'She died,' he says quietly. I grope for words of commiseration. But words are inadequate. Sometimes silence speaks. He seems grateful for the silence.

'And you?' he asks a while later.

'There was someone I once loved.' I say it matter-of-factly, ignoring the sudden spasm I feel in my chest. The heart does ache, I think with surprise.

'What happened?' His voice is more polite than curious. Love affairs are commonplace. They evoke no interest.

'She didn't.' I chuckle. Only I can hear the pathos in my voice. He can't even fathom it. 'It was a long time ago,' I add. I do not lie. Sometimes a year and a half constitute a lifetime.

I attempt a smile. I do not want him to pity me. He smiles as well. After dinner, I walk back with him to his house. The house is impressive from the outside. I think of my tiny two-bedroom apartment. Many would call it cramped. I call it compact. But our lives are different, Nishant's and mine.

He has grown roots here, while I am merely a bird of passage.

We stand outside his house, but he does not invite me inside.

'I had to redo my house,' he says. 'There was a fire, not so long ago.'

It must have been more than four months ago. I have been here for four months. I think the memories of the fire still haunt him. He is not ready to say anything else about it. I wonder what burnt in the fire. Some day, when he wants to confide in me, he will. Until then, I must respect his privacy. Anyway, all that is in the past. We all have a past. Some have an uglier past than others. I leave him at the gate and walk back.

Fifteen minutes later, I am standing on my balcony. The faint smell of jasmine seeps in. I inhale the sweet smell slowly. It reminds me of Shailaja. I close my eyes and she is before me, her hair falling all over her face, which she brushes aside carelessly with her hand. I love her hair. I love her face. I love the way her eyes dart about curiously. I love the way she pouts unselfconsciously when things don't go her way. I love everything about her.

I close my eyes and the years roll away.

I fell in love with Shailaja when I saw her for the first time in the operation theatre, when her leg was being operated upon. I have loved her ever since. I am nothing if not stable in my emotions. 'Just count up to ten,' I told her in a soft voice, 'and you will be asleep before you're done.' She smiled at me; her eyes as bright as stars on a moonlit night. The nurse in the operation theatre, Zeenat, saw me staring at her and smiled. She teased me for days after that.

I met Shailaja many times after that, although I was not her surgeon. I met her every time she came to the hospital for a follow-up and when she came for physiotherapy. I even visited her at home. We became friends. We were 'just friends', the euphemism Indians use when they are in a relationship. There were times I wanted to express my feelings but couldn't. There is a time for everything, I told myself. My time will come. One day, I invited her home for a meal. I didn't think she would I agree. But she did. Fortune favours the brave, I thought exultantly.

'Sit,' I said, as excited as a schoolboy when I first saw her at home. I was no longer a doctor. I was a schoolboy in front of his first crush. And then, the words I wanted to say but couldn't before, came out miraculously. 'I love you.' It is not really a tongue twister. I said it without faltering. 'I want to marry you.' There. I had said it at last. She seemed amused. And touched.

'I am sorry,' she said kindly, 'I can't. There is someone else.' I heard something break. It was only the glass I was holding in my hand. As I bent down to pick up the shards, one pricked my finger. I bled. *'How appropriate,'* I had thought, *'hearts do bleed.'* She left soon after the meal without realizing the devastation she had wrought with her words. Words can be powerful weapons. They can destroy.

The next I heard was that she was married. It was an arranged marriage. Dammit, I thought. She left me due to familial pressures. 'The someone else' she had referred to was probably someone chosen by her balding, eagle-eyed father with his patrician nose, or maybe by her brother, who was a pale imitation of his father. She had been forced into an arranged marriage. She had disappeared from my life. A year later, I left Delhi. They say a change of place helps one heal.

I meet Nishant at work every day, and slowly, our friendship grows, as it is bound to. We are two men, both doctors, both single, working together in a small town. I realize just how small the town is when I take a round of it in my Volkswagen Polo. Delhi can swallow ten such towns. Or maybe twenty. Nishant and I meet frequently. We have much in common, apart from our work. Our love for books and chess. Our love for music. He sings. I play the sitar. We differ in many ways. He is a vegetarian. I love chicken and fish. We differ in our views on love and marriage. He abhors gay relationships. I don't. When we talk about them, he shudders. He is homophobic.

'Love is love,' I say, 'you can't keep it under wraps.'

One day, he is ready to talk about his wife. I knew the time would come.

'It was an accident,' he tells me, when he finally invites me to his house for dinner, 'an LPG gas explosion.'

'She ... did not smell the gas?' I express my surprise.

We both know that liquified petroleum gas is odourless and that ethyl mercaptan is added to it so that the gas can be detected during a leak. She must be suffering from anosmia, possibly congenital anosmia, the loss of sense of smell.

'She deserved it,' he says harshly under his breath, but I can hear him. I look at him quizzically. He cannot withdraw the words he has uttered so inadvertently. He flushes. 'I caught her with someone else.'

'With another man?' I ask, my voice commiserating.

'With another woman,' he swears under his breath. I look at him. I see a faint smile on his face. It is gone a moment later. Perhaps I imagined it. I can guess what happened. Nishant knew his wife was having an affair and he killed her. He must have known that she suffered from anosmia. She could not smell the leaking gas. He must have known that his unsuspecting wife would make a cup of tea or something for herself and burn like a flame.

I close my eyes and think of Nishant's wife. Shailaja. The woman I loved. I think of her friend, Zeenat, the nurse at my hospital, back in Delhi.

Both Zeenat and I had seen Shailaja in the operation theatre on the day of her operation. Zeenat won. I lost. Shailaja must have used me as a foil. No one would have guessed anything about her relationship with Zeenat if she was seen with me.

She had used me, but somehow I could not blame her. Now I knew why her father had rushed her into a marriage. He must have guessed at the truth.

Zeenat used to come from Delhi and meet Shailaja on her weekly off day. Nishant must have returned home one afternoon and seen them together. After all, he had a key to the house. Was that when he planned his revenge? Did he cut the gas pipe himself? It was all so simple. He must have planned to kill them both. Zeenat had escaped—miraculously, because she had been caught in a traffic jam. Providence. I must learn to believe in it.

I close my eyes once again and Zeenat stands before me. Shaken. Broken. Seeking justice for Shailaja.

'It must have been an accident,' I say. 'No man would do something like that to his wife.'

'You do not know Nishant,' she says. Zeenat has Shailaja's diary. She reads out excerpts from it. I learn about Nishant's suspicious nature, about his violence towards Shailaja, about the scars she carried on her body. I learn about his locking Shailaja up at home at times, and only allowing Zeenat to meet her, because she was a woman. 'He must have seen us together ...' she admits. She leaves a lot unsaid.

'You must find a job in his hospital and learn the truth,' she says.

'And leave my job here?' I ask incredulously.

'I thought you loved her,' she pleads, 'and you know that you can get your old job back any time you want.' I close my eyes and I see not the Shailaja with her windswept hair and luminescent smile whom I loved, but the Shailaja burnt from head to toe, writhing in agony, whom I do not know at all.

'It will take me months to befriend him,' I caution.

'I'll wait,' she says.

Six months later, I meet Zeenat in Delhi.

'What next?' I ask.

'If you succeed in bringing him to the Police Headquarters office, I will take care of everything,' she says.

'The death isn't within the jurisdiction of Delhi Police,' I begin to protest.

'It is,' she says. 'Shailaja did not die in her house. She sustained ninety per cent burns and she was brought to the Safdarjung Hospital Burns Unit in New Delhi. She died the next day.' Safdarjung Hospital Burns Unit. The best Burns Unit in the capital, and possibly in the country. But what could they do? They are not miracle workers.

'So, the jurisdiction is Delhi,' she says, nodding her head vehemently, 'and my cousin's husband is the Commissioner of Police.'

Bringing Nishant to Delhi will not be easy. But I have to try. For Shailaja's sake. I try to imagine Shailaja sustaining ninety per cent burns, her body charred, writhing in agony, craving water, craving for respite from the pain once the effects of morphine wore off. Knowing that she was going to die. Thinking that her killer would go unpunished. Zeenat is right. Shailaja deserves justice. I cannot let her become a forgotten chapter in Nishant's life, the man with no remorse.

'Why are we going?' asks Nishant petulantly as I bundle him into my car on a Saturday.

'It's my birthday and I want to celebrate,' I say in a voice which will brook no arguments.

'Why not celebrate here?' he asks.

'Here?' I wrinkle my nose. 'In this village? Let's go to Delhi.'

'I am tired, I have just performed a four-hour-long surgery,' he argues. 'I am about to fall asleep.'

I can see that he is on the verge of collapse. I need him to be exhausted. I need him to sleep on the way so that he wakes up only when we reach our destination. The rest is in Zeenat's hands.

'You need to relax. Why don't you sleep in the car?' I say, 'I will let you know when we reach the city.'

He agrees, gets into the car and goes to sleep almost immediately. I feel guilty for betraying a colleague. Then, I think of Shailaja, and I no longer feel a shred of guilt.

The Outsider

'Wearing the carpet down,' I murmur, as I see a young father-to-be pacing up and down the corridor. 'So are you, my friend,' I add to myself. The carpet is metaphorical. All I see before me is a scrubbed, mosaic floor. The witching hour has passed. It is 12.15 a.m. now. Why do children choose inconvenient times to be born? 'What begins at night, ends at night,' I have heard people murmur this trite phrase repeatedly. Perhaps that is true. I wouldn't know. I am inexperienced in these matters.

'Your first?' someone asks as he passes by. I mutter something incoherently. The man nods his head. No one is actually interested in the answer.

A nurse walks into the waiting room. Her glance sweeps across the room. Then she walks purposefully towards me. 'Mr Sahay?' she inquires.

I look at her blankly. Then it registers. She is addressing me. Perhaps she has seen me, with Aarti leaning on my shoulder as I rushed her into the hospital. I nod.

'Congratulations, it's a boy.' She beams. 'You can see her now,' she adds. She means Aarti.

'Er, by the way ... I am not ...' I begin to say, but she is already striding ahead. I give up. There will be time enough for explanations later.

I walk into the post-delivery room. Aarti is lying with her eyes closed, looking wan. This is how she looked when she had fallen from the mango tree in her garden, so many years ago. For a few heart-stopping moments I had thought that she had stopped breathing. Then she had opened her eyes and I had begun to breathe once more. This time, I realize, she is merely exhausted.

Aarti opens her eyes.

'How are you feeling?' I ask.

'I feel exhausted,' she says, 'as though I have climbed a mountain. I wonder how women actually had eight or nine children.' She shudders and I laugh. If Aarti has her way, Junior will be an only child. The nurse looks at me indulgently and then guides me towards the crib.

'You can hold the baby,' she says, 'before I take him to the nursery.' I lift the baby into my arms gingerly. My hands are shaking. I cannot recollect when I last held a newborn baby. For a moment I stop breathing. I cannot get over the wonder of it all. After a minute, I hand over the baby to the nurse and return to the waiting room.

I spy a coffee dispenser nearby. Thank goodness for coffee, the one stimulant that keeps me awake. I take a sip. It burns my tongue. I am likely to stay awake the whole night. Actually, I need to. I have to make a presentation tomorrow afternoon. I hate to think what my boss will say if I take a holiday tomorrow. He will have an apoplectic fit if I am not there. For him, nothing can come in the way of this presentation. Not even the birth of a child. But it is nice to feel indispensable at times.

I begin to feel peckish. Stress always makes me hungry. I saunter down the corridor, looking for something to eat. It's a forlorn hope. Where can I find food at 1.10 a.m. except at a railway station? But it seems that today is my lucky day. I find a vending machine dispensing chips and nachos. I choose a packet: Ruffles Lays Classic Salted chips.

The packaged chips transport me back into my childhood. Not all childhood memories are pleasant. Mine certainly aren't. A deprived childhood makes for painful memories. The chips remind me of birthdays, especially children's birthdays. Aarti's birthday, for instance, to which I, her father's employee's son, was invited only because I was her classmate. I usually stood in a corner, looking covetously at the table that was groaning under food, wishing that my birthday could be celebrated with the same gusto.

I return to the waiting room sofa and watch the other man continue his pacing. His wife must be having a difficult labour. A little while later, the nurse comes in. 'It's a girl,' she says non-committally to the man. She doesn't know how the news will be received.

'Whoopee!' he says, exultation all over his face, catching the nurse by her shoulders. She is surprised. She must rarely have had the birth of a daughter received with so much enthusiasm. He lets go of her, embarrassed by his impulses. 'I already have twin sons,' he says by way of explanation.

I smile and turn towards the hallway. My eyes widen with surprise as I see a familiar middle-aged woman emerge from the lift. She makes a beeline for me and grips me by my shoulders.

'How is Aarti?' she demands. I wince.

For a fifty-five-year-old, Smita Aunty has a very powerful grip.

'Aarti is fine,' I say. I see the quizzical look on her face. 'It's a boy,' I add. She grips my shoulders once again and beams. She belongs to the old school; for her, boys are always more welcome than girls. I see her hurry down towards the post-delivery room. Now that she is here, I can go home and work on my presentation, and if I am lucky, get some sleep. She looks crestfallen when she learns that I am leaving.

'You will come tomorrow,' she says.

I wonder if it is a question or a command.

'After work,' I murmur.

The presentation goes well, as well as it can with four hours of preparation and four hours of sleep. I return to the hospital at 6 p.m. wondering if I will be allowed in. Thank goodness the visiting hours are from 6 to 7 p.m.

'You took your time,' says Smita Aunty when she sees me, a trifle gruffly.

'She missed her errand boy,' Aarti laughs. Aunty flushes. So do I. Probably that is what I have always been to her: an errand boy. The son of her husband's employee who hung around her house and was always at her beck and call. However high I rise up the corporate ladder, I will always be her errand boy; even if I become the CEO of the company I work in. The day before, she had made a frantic call to me.

'Aarti's water bag broke,' she had said imperiously on the phone. I could not figure out what she meant by it. I am a bachelor after all. 'Rush her to the Diwan Nursing Home,' she had added impatiently.

'Aarti is all alone. She is in labour,' she explained when I said nothing. I had looked wistfully at the presentation I had begun to work on. But I knew my priorities. Babies don't wait. Even I knew that. I was at Aarti's house within fifteen minutes, jumping a few traffic lights on the way and Aarti was at the nursing home within an hour.

The nurse comes in and smiles at me. She leads me to the crib, and once again, she hands over the baby to me. This time, I hold the baby more confidently and tell Aarti, 'He looks just like his father.'

'Not even a bit like me?' She laughs.

Just then, Vivek walks into the room. I have never met him before. But I know instinctively who he is—Aarti's husband who lives in Dubai. He must have booked his ticket for the earliest available flight once he heard the news. He must have come straight from the airport. His hair is dishevelled and he looks tired.

'Who is he?' The nurse nudges me curiously.

'I am her husband,' he says, his voice brusque.

'Then who are you?' she asks, looking over at me speculatively. Vivek raises his eyebrows. He has never met me before. He probably wonders why the nurse mistook me to be Aarti's husband. Everyone starts talking at once. 'He is Aseem Kulshreshtha, Aarti's childhood friend,' says Smita Aunty. 'He's just a friend,' says Aarti off-handedly, 'who brought me here.'

'I came to get Aarti admitted into the hospital because it was an emergency and there was no family member around,' I mumble.

'I see,' says the nurse drily. But it is clear that she does not see. She is riled by the fact that last night I let her assume that I was Aarti's husband when I had had all the time in the world to tell her otherwise.

'Never saw you at our wedding,' Vivek Sahay says, his voice suspicious. Maybe it is not easy to build trust while in a long-distance marriage, especially if it is an arranged one, and Vivek and Aarti have been married for less than two years.

'I was away on a business trip,' I say.

His face still looks grim. This does not augur well for Aarti. Some men are suspicious. I guess Vivek is. Why did Aarti marry him? I begin to pity her.

Aunty invites me for the sixth day, ceremony; it is called 'chatti' in our community. I go to Aarti's house in Defence Colony. I can see the pandit getting ready to perform the havan and I can hear raised voices from a room nearby. It is a pity that modern houses have such painfully thin walls.

'I want a DNA test.' That must be Vivek.

'Why?'

'Well, what are DNA tests for? To prove paternity. After all, I do not live in India. I live in Dubai while you live here. I only come for short visits…..' He leaves the sentence hanging but the implications of his words are clear.

'You are accusing me of adultery,' remarks Aarti dully.

'No, just setting my mind at rest.'

'I won't do it.'

'What do you have to hide?'

Just how crass can Vivek get? If I were in Aarti's place I would have kicked him out. Instead, I hear Aarti's defeated voice.

'Okay.'

Marriage takes the courage out of a person, I realize. I knew Aarti to be a feisty lawyer, full of spunk. I wonder if I should leave the premises. A minute later, they walk out of their room.

Aarti is holding the baby while Vivek's arm is draped tenderly around Aarti.

'What a performance,' I think cynically. They deserve a standing ovation for it. The pandit begins the puja. When it is over, I leave without a goodbye.

It has been a month since Aarav was born. To celebrate his birth, Aarti and Vivek are holding a party. I am early. No, I am on time. It is not my fault that everyone else is late.

The celebrations begin late and continue into the night. I am the last to leave, not simply because I wanted to linger, but because Smita Aunty likes to have her errand boy around.

Aarti comes into the drawing room just as I am about to leave. She ignores me. She is clutching something in her hand. A report. She hands it to Vivek. He sees it. His face changes. A look of indescribable joy sweeps over his face. He goes to the crib, picks up the baby and smothers him with kisses.

'My son, my son,' he says, over and over again.

Aarti stares at him quizzically. I wonder what she's thinking; it is impossible to know. I could never figure out what she was thinking, even though we had grown up together. She can be so enigmatic. She lets Vivek exult in the moment. It is a moment she does not want to snatch away from him.

Then, she speaks. 'Vivek, I have done what you wanted. Now I want something in exchange.'

'Whatever you want,' he says. He has never looked at her so tenderly before.

'My freedom.'

'Freedom?' He doesn't understand. '… What do you mean?'

'A divorce,' she says baldly.

'Divorce? Why?' He raises his eyebrows. She has stolen his

line. This is what he had expected to say to her after receiving the DNA test results.

'But why ... now that you have proved ...?'

'That Aarav is not a bastard.' Her voice is harsh. I can hear the raw pain in it. 'The test was to prove to you that Aarav was your son, and not a bastard. I need my freedom, to bring him up in a non-toxic atmosphere so that he grows up to be a human being.' Aarti can be quite vitriolic when she wants.

'Aarti—' Vivek falters. I could have spoken up before. Told Vivek not to mess with Aarti. She walks away, her back ramrod straight. I see Vivek, his shoulders slowly drooping. My heart begins to beat loudly. Aarti still sees me as a friend, a good friend. I have never seen her as a friend. She is the girl I love and have loved all my life. People change. Feelings change. Aarti may also change.

Once again, I begin to hope.

Breaking Barriers

At times, people remind me of vultures, those scavenging birds with talons that tear into the flesh of the dead on top of the Dakhma. Thank God we are not Zoroastrians. We do not leave the bodies of our dead on the Dakhma, the Tower of Silence, for vultures to devour. We are Hindus. Traditional, tied down by rites and rituals, where men wear the sacred thread or janeu across their chests and women are saree clad after marriage, a streak of vermilion colouring their foreheads. But that does not stop us from being vultures either.

'When is he coming?' inquires my aunt. She is referring obliquely to my brother, Amitabh. Aunt Saraswati chooses not to take his name, in deference to the fact that, although Amitabh is two years younger than me, according to her, he now heads our household. Indians are like that. Bound by religion, nurtured in tradition, unable to break out of the mould.

Mother lies on a slab of ice. I have put the air conditioner on. Normally, we use it only for a few hours every day, to keep the electricity bills low. But this is an emergency. Summer is not a good time to die. Why could she not have chosen winter? Then I wouldn't have to scrounge around the city for ice and pay exorbitant electricity bills. I chuckle softly. Even in the midst of grief my sense of humour has not deserted me.

Mother looks as beautiful in death as she had in life. For the cremation she will be dressed in a stunning white and gold saree. She will look even more beautiful. Maybe I am biased. I love my mother. I do not see her wrinkled skin and gnarled hands. I see the smile which used to light up her face. I think I can still see it on her face. Maybe I am imagining it.

Someone enters the room. My uncle, Dinesh.

'So, when will Amitabh arrive?' He is more direct. Men in India think that they can rule the world, or at least our lives. But there is a reason for his impatience. We have a cremation to perform. Mother died yesterday morning. We could have cremated her yesterday. But we are waiting for Amitabh to arrive.

I ignore Uncle Dinesh. I pour myself a cup of tea from a thermos flask and set it on the side table. It is from a nearby tea stall. It is overly sweet and tastes of ginger, cloves and cardamom. I place a plate containing four cream cracker biscuits with slivers of cheese on them, next to the tea. This is to be my breakfast. Normally, I would have made an egg white omelette, with onions, tomatoes, green chillies and cheese, but in our community, non-vegetarian food is taboo when someone dies. In any case, the kitchen stove is not lit until the dead is cremated and the prayer meeting held. Till then, one is at the mercy of friends and relations, who bring food for the family.

I am feeling claustrophobic in my own home. I do not suffer from claustrophobia. But then, I have never had twenty people inside my two-bedroom house before. Thank goodness nobody has asked me for anything. They really can't. No cooking is allowed anyway. Besides, one is supposed to lose one's appetite during a tragedy. I do not need to apologize to anyone in case they feel famished.

I look through my emails. My messages. My WhatsApp messages. There is no word from Amitabh. He had said yesterday that he would arrive this morning. Switzerland is not New York. It is only eleven hours away. And this is an emergency. Even the airlines would have helped.

Amitabh has been away from India for ten years. No, make that fifteen. It is strange how, after a while, we lose track of time. I have been tied to this house for fifteen years. He has Emma by his side. I have no one. I am a spinster. He is on Facetime with us quite often, flaunting his children, Nick and Tamara. I have Mother. Correction. I had Mother. He thinks that the paltry twenty minutes of Facetime every fortnight absolves him of the responsibility of looking after his mother. I don't. He thinks she didn't need any financial help because she received 30,000 rupees as father's family pension. I disagree. He thinks I am a spinster by choice. I think I am one by circumstance.

Amitabh is an engineer by profession. I think I should have been one. I was brighter, academically. But I was the wrong sex. 'We can only afford to send one child to engineering college,' Father had said. It was clear that it would be Amitabh, the preferred child, while I would do my MSc in chemistry. I joined government service not because I wanted to, but because father decided that it would give me stability and security, while Amitabh winged his way to the US to live out his dreams. I call it a classic case of gender discrimination.

I have a list of grievances. I take them out and air them occasionally. It gives me great relief. Grievances, once articulated, clear the air. Grievances, bottled up, become festering sores. Mother is dead. That is my only reality. When she died yesterday, I cried with relief. At last, it was over. She would no longer linger, cling on to life, when she was better dead. She clung on, despite the fact that her left body was paralysed, so that she could see Amitabh and the grandchildren. She didn't care much for Emma. But Amitabh was away. They were holidaying in the salubrious climes of Switzerland, travelling to Zermatt to see Matterhorn, going to Interlaken and Geneva, Zurich and Lucerne—all while Mother was dying. Amitabh has his priorities—Emma, Nick and Tamara. In that order. Mother came afterwards. That is why he missed the fortnightly chat with me. That is why his mobile remained switched off for the duration of his vacation. Perhaps he kept his official phone on, but I have no access to it. That was why he did not access his emails. That is why he did not know of the stroke Mother had suffered from fifteen days before she passed away.

'At least she didn't suffer for too long.' Amitabh is very good at mouthing such platitudes. I wish I had such a gift.

Suddenly, I hear a ping on my phone.

'Defer cremation. Can't arrive today. Will arrive tomorrow.'

Defer cremation? What does Amitabh mean? I have already deferred it by a day. Where will we keep the body? *How* will we keep the body? I have no idea.

This is the first time that I am dealing with a death in the family. Mother had taken care of Father's cremation. I am not an expert in these matters. Just what does he mean? How can he be so presumptuous? He thinks that he can snap his fingers and we will run around doing his bidding. He must be lounging in his hotel room in Interlaken, which he assures me is heaven, surrounded as it is by lush green woods and snow-capped mountains.

I sit in my chair, contemplative, my tea nearly finished. How do I resolve the issue of the cremation? My uncle, Dinesh, looks through me, dismissive. I am forty-three years old. I work in a pokey little office, pushing files. He does not think much of me. People have strange notions about junior bureaucrats.

Outside, I can hear women wailing. Lamenting a death is a tradition in India. Earlier, women would beat their chests and wail loudly. Nowadays, most women cry quietly into their handkerchiefs. But the women who are weeping in the drawing room belong to Mother's generation. They continue to wail loudly.

I pick up the newspaper and glance at the front page idly. I scan the headlines. The Delhi High Court has declared that the daughter too can be a manager in a Hindu Undivided Family. We are, of course, a nuclear family. 'The daughter has property rights equal to a son. She has an equal share in the family's ancestral property, including the agricultural property,' I read. This has been true since 2005, in fact. I didn't know this. I think of our ancestral house and the farm. I thought it all belonged to Amitabh. It doesn't. I have an equal share in it. I am appalled by my own ignorance. By implication, a daughter can also perform a cremation. I read the article twice. I look at my watch. It is only 8.30 a.m. I ring up Nigambodh Ghat, the oldest cremation ground in Delhi, and confirm that the cremation will be held at noon.

'Inform everybody that the cremation is to be at 12 noon,' I command Dinesh Uncle. At the same time, I begin messaging my relatives who are not present. They all know the cremation will be held today; they don't know the time until I tell them.

Dinesh Uncle is shocked. He has never heard me speak so firmly. We reach the cremation grounds by 11.30 a.m. The preparations for the cremation begin.

'Where is Amitabh?' asks Dinesh Uncle.

'In Switzerland,' I say.

'Then who will perform the cremation?' he questions, his eyebrows raised.

'I will,' I respond. He is horrified.

'You can't do it,' he shouts, 'you are a woman, a daughter, only a son can perform the cremation.'

I turn to the priest. 'What do the scriptures say?'

'The scriptures say the offspring should perform it,' the priest confirms.

'So, I can perform it,' I reply. 'I am the elder offspring.' There is triumph in my voice.

'But ... you have a brother,' says Dinesh Uncle, as though this fact will put an end to all my arguments.

'So did Mallika Sarabhai,' I say, referring to the multi-talented danseuse, whose father, the late Dr Vikram Sarabhai, was considered the father of the space programme in India. 'She had an older brother, Kartikeya, who was in Cambridge and could not come to India in time. So, she performed the cremation.'

'I don't remember reading about it in the newspapers,' Dinesh Uncle says aggressively.

'I am not responsible for your ignorance,' I respond. The look of consternation on his face makes me laugh.

'It happened years ago,' I say gently, 'forty-five years to be precise.'

All the decisions in my life have been made by others. It is time I made my own. I pick up the earthen pot brimming with water and begin walking, around Mother's pyre. I perform the ritual and then, with heft, break the pot on the floor. I pick up the stick. This is the really tough part, the kapal kriya.

I have to break open my mother's skull, to ensure that her body burns easily and that her soul is released from her body. The priest looks at me intently. He knows that this can be difficult, even traumatic. I am 5'5" tall. Will I even be able to do it?

I pick up the bamboo stick and tighten my hold on it. In a flash, I think of all I deserve and all that I have been denied. My quota of happiness that Amitabh stole, my ambitions which Father thwarted while my mother stood like a silent bystander all through, not willing to take sides. It must be my anger which gives me the strength. Her skull cracks open in the first blow. I have to repeat the ritual two more times. Reaction sets in. I break into sobs. Loud gut-wrenching sobs. I had been dry-eyed till now. I feel terribly fatigued. But I know, this is a turning point in my life. This is the first tradition I have broken. There are many more I have to break.

Guilt

There is an air about dusk that makes me nervous. I step out of the house at 5.45 p.m. The sun has disappeared below but the weather is pleasant. I glance at my mi fit band and make a face. The day is nearly over and I have taken only 1100 steps. I wish I had gone for my morning walk. Morning walks are far more invigorating that evening walks. There is a soft glow in the sky and a nip in the air, I think but then check myself. Who am I deluding? The air in Delhi is so toxic that people have been advised to avoid an early morning walk.

That is the reason for my change of routine. At least, that is how I convince myself.

I need to take a round of the entire colony to complete my daily quota. Vasant Kunj is notorious for thefts, particularly car thefts. I do not feel safe; but I persist. I walk past the community centre towards gate number five, turning and intently searching for something behind me. One must be wary of dogs. They bite. The fragrance of roses wafts towards me. An amateur gardener has several pots of roses in her garden. I smile. I wish I had green fingers.

I turn towards the park. There are many parks in the colony, but this is the largest one. It has been renovated recently. Many new exercise machines have been installed. There are exercycles, steppers and rowing machines. Even exercise bars have been put up.

I cross the park and peer into the apartment blocks. This is a new obsession of mine. The DDA has now allowed blocks of flats to have lifts installed. I try to see how many house owners have taken up this offer and installed lifts. Very few, I realize. I can count only two. I reach the commercial complex in the colony. There are two dry cleaner shops, two grocery stores and two pharmacies in the complex. There is also a restaurant on the first floor, called Orient Tavern. I have never been there. I am told it is more of a bar than a restaurant. There is a Safal store and a Mother Diary booth nearby. We even have an ATM within the complex.

'Quite self-sufficient,' I muse.

I stride towards the walkers' path. As I walk back home, I begin to feel tired. I sit on the bench in the shelter constructed by the Resident Welfare Association.

He is already sitting there, a cricket cap on his head. Is it really that hot or is this a disguise? He smiles. It is dusk now. The fan in the shelter is whirring loudly. I wipe my face with my dupatta, glad that I have doused myself with my favourite perfume, Vanilla, bought at Bodyshop. It is not a patch on Chanel No. 5, but it is pleasant. I feel like a housewife who has just finished baking a cake.

He clears his throat. 'How have you been?'

I smile into the darkness.

'Not much has changed between yesterday and today,' I say lightly.

He laughs a little at my repartee. 'Witty,' he says.

'You mean caustic,' I rejoin. He smiles, or I think he does. It is difficult to see in the dark.

We sit in silence, not because we have run out of conversation but because it is companionable.

After a while, I say, 'Have you seen the film *Maroon*? It's on Netflix. It made no sense to me.'

'No, but I saw *Game Over*,' he says, 'I couldn't understand that either.'

We both laugh. Netflix has turned us both into couch potatoes. Suddenly, he looks up and asks, 'Care for a cup of coffee?'

This is progress. We have been sitting in companionable silence for the past two weeks, but he has never asked me out. I wish that I had the foresight to carry a scarf with me for camouflage. 'I make good coffee,' he says. Thank goodness we are not going out. He gets up. I follow him.

'Has this been the pattern of my life?' I wonder. I walk slowly behind him, wondering in which block and on which floor he lives. All this while, we have talked at the shelter. I have never asked him about it. Somehow, it seemed too personal. He turns towards the Park. His house is on the first floor. Thank goodness. It makes for a little anonymity. His flat is the right one. It faces the east. According to vaastu, that is lucky. Although I am sure he had no say in the matter. DDA flats are allotted by lottery. I sit in the drawing room. If I had to choose one word to describe the decor, I would have said it was 'spartan.' There is nothing in the drawing room to tell me about the man himself. No photographs of loved ones, parents or wife or children. There is a solitary painting on the wall. It is beautiful. Has he painted it himself? I squint but can't see

if there is a signature on the canvas. There is a stained-glass lamp on a side table.

'Classy,' I say in an undertone.

The walls are painted grey and pink, an unusual colour combination. Then, I spot a bookshelf. I realize that I am wrong. The room does tell me a lot about him. A man is known by the books he reads. It is an eclectic collection on display: *Gone with the Wind, Remains of the Day, An English Patient*, books by Sidney Sheldon, Frederick Forsyth and Jeffrey Archer. At least he reads.

Subir is a doctor, a dermatologist. I had consulted with him for a skin problem I had developed suddenly and his ointment had worked wonders. A month later, I met him during my evening walk. Well, friendships start in the most unobtrusive of ways.

He returns to the room with two cups of steaming coffee and a plate of chocolate chip cookies. 'My favourite,' he declares. I take a sip. The coffee is perfect. It reeks of old memories; of sand-strewn beaches, garden umbrellas and jars of brew, of snow-clad winters and warm blankets with mugs of strong black coffee. Suddenly, I feel his fingertips on mine. I sit still. Maybe it was inadvertent. It happens again. I recoil.

'I'm sorry,' he says quickly.

'I'm sorry,' I mutter.

Why am I behaving like a schoolgirl? It was only an accidental touch, for god's sake. Or was it? I am not sure. Does he think that because I am a widow, I am available? I hope I am wrong. I finish my coffee slowly, smile at him and look at my watch.

'Oh my God, I'm really late,' I exclaim suddenly. I hope

to hear him say, 'Stay back for a little longer', but he doesn't. It really is getting late. It is 7 p.m. now. Usually, I'm home by 6.30 p.m.

I leave, gently closing the door behind me. I turn towards my flat. It is on the ground floor. I ring the bell. Sunanda opens the door.

'Hi! Had a good walk?' she asks. 'Come inside,' she says. 'You must be tired. I'll make you a cup of tea.'

She makes me a cup of tea every day at 6.30 p.m., and yet she doesn't ask me why I am late on this particular evening. She is not judgemental. Her eyes are kind. But I think she can read my mind; she definitely notices my flushed cheeks. Shikhar comes in after me. He is swinging a cricket bat in his hand. He must have been playing street cricket. He is still wary of me. We have not known each other for too long. I am glad that he is not openly hostile.

'What do you want, young man?' Sunanda asks him.

'Chocolate chip cookies,' he announces.

I gulp.

I look at the photos on the wall. I see the photograph of my husband, Sudeep, who died of a stroke, only six months ago. He was not conventionally good-looking, but he had a craggy, interesting face, and eyes that twinkled all the time. He was sixty-two when he died. But, as he used to say, chartered accountants have no retirement age; they only collapse on their desk from exhaustion and overwork.

Then I look at my son, Shantanu, wearing his Air Force uniform, who died when his MIG crashed, seven years ago. He was the handsome one. I was heart-broken when he died. Thankfully, I had Sudeep by my side. I wept on his shoulder for days until the tears dried. Together we weathered the storm. We left Sunanda to cope with her own sorrow because she was a doctor; everyone knows that doctors are resilient. Also, somehow, we could never accept her as Shantanu's wife. After all, he had married her without our blessings.

Seven years later, Sudeep died and Sunanda flew to Bhopal with Shikhar, who performed the last rites for his grandfather. She insisted on locking up the house and taking me with her to Delhi. 'The house will haunt you and you will sink into depression. Believe me, I know. I am a doctor *and* I have been there.' There is no reproach in her voice at all, but I am overcome with shame.

My arm tingled when Subir's fingers touched me, and I am fifty-eight. I still yearn for Sudeep at times. Does Sunanda not long for a man's touch? She's just thirty-seven years old. How does she cope? Does she still miss Shantanu after all this time? Does she not yearn for a man? I have never thought about her, so wrapped have I been in my own grief.

Her eyes are still kind. She brings me a mug of tea, cardamom infused. 'I have put stevia in it,' she says. 'Well,' she adds, handing me my cup, 'I know that you are not diabetic, but there is no harm in taking precautions.' Along with the tea she has brought a plate of Threptin biscuits.

'They are not chocolate chip cookies,' she says mischievously as she brushes the crumbs of chocolate chip cookies from my dupatta, 'but you need your protein.' I gulp the cardamom-infused tea and hope that it will wash away the rancid taste of coffee from my mouth.

Ring of Fire

I had a nightmare again. Or is it better described as a dream? I cannot distinguish between the two. All I see is a smudged, sepia-coloured photograph of an age-dimmed past, browning at the edges. I see a boy, holding the hand of a man with brown hair, and a fairy. Then the man and the fairy disappear, and he is left all alone. The photograph turns orange. Like the flame of the forest. I have had the same dream many times before. Then it was in monochrome.

I wake up, my face drenched in sweat, my throat parched and lips cracked.

'Welcome to the enervating heat of the Indian summer,' I murmur sardonically.

I groan as I look at the time. School begins in an hour. My back aches. My hair is singed. I dip my fingers into the tin of coconut oil next to the bed and rub them against my back. It soothes my skin. Just how did I manage to burn myself yesterday? Haven't I glided through the ring of fire thousands of times before?

Practice makes perfect. But one minute of distraction, and one is undone. Luckily, practice has taught me to accept pain without a grimace. No one but I realized that I had been scorched.

Pain is an inevitable part of life. Life simply must go on. Had I made a fuss, someone in the audience would have noticed and then Rahim Chacha would have had to pay the price, maybe even stop the street circus from performing ever again. But I have to keep the home fires burning, even if I am only fourteen years old and 'child labour' is banned in India. But the street circus is the only thing I know, as did my father.

Every day, I rub myself with oil and when my turn comes, I jump and glide through the 'Ring of Fire'. There is no resounding applause for me. Street artists do not receive such appreciation. Over the years, I have learnt to glide safely through the blaze of the fire. Not once but twice, and at times, even six times. Because for the audience, once is not enough. Everyone says I am a hero, but I think Salma is the real hero. Perched precariously on a rope while holding on to a pole, she moves. She balances herself on the tightrope until she reaches the end. I have tried it and have failed. I could only go to the halfway point, but then I toppled down. How does she remain undeterred by the crowd and their comments? How can she withstand the cheering and the jeering? How can she concentrate? Does she chant mantras secretly? Salma doesn't tell.

Every troupe artist has his trade secret. I know why. I have heard about the incident. So has every street artist. I do not know if the legend is real or apocryphal, but it makes for a great story anyway. I smile. I am a cynic at heart. The story concerns the globe of death. I have heard that it is a contraption made out of steel, circular in shape, in which a rider sits astride his motorcycle and drives at an increasingly faster speed. I have never seen it being performed. I have never seen a circus.

To go on with the story, the man performed the death-defying feat, night after night, while making his beloved sit on the same seat in the audience every night. She thought it was because he wanted her to have a ringside view of his act. But he confessed to her that he concentrated upon her when he rode, and he commanded her to never move during his act. She did his bidding, until one day, just as his motorcycle picked up speed and as it zoomed up and down the globe, she got up and moved away. Then, she smiled. Okay, I admit, I cannot speak with certainty about the smile. I made it up. The motorcyclist crashed and died. All circus artists know that they should keep their trade secrets close to their chest so that no one can betray their confidence. No one is to be trusted, especially not lovers.

Perhaps that is why Rahul and Robin, who perform the dagger act, have never disclosed their secret either, not even to each other. They are even more daring than Salma. I have seen Rahul throw knife after knife, with unfailing accuracy, while Robin stays still on the floor, immobile as the knives land above his forehead, near his neck and by his ear. He remains so still he could very well be dead. How do they do it? How does Rahul throw the knives with unfailing accuracy? How does Robin stay still? How come he never gets injured? Are the knives fake? I do not know.

Rahul and Robin do not tell. Every artist has his trade secret.

'Still daydreaming?' my mother asks. 'Get ready for school.'

Mother is a tyrant. Perhaps all mothers are. I go outside the house, fill my bucket with water and then pour the water over my head. The water, icy-cold, dribbles down my back and I stand, shell-shocked. How does the well water remain so cool, even in the blistering heat? I must ask my science teacher. I gather the little pieces of soap in the soap case and lather myself with them. A little later, I am ready for school.

I sit cross-legged on the jute mat, and tuck into the breakfast Mother places before me. It is leftover rice, soaked overnight in water with slices of onion, green chillies and salt in it. Ma has even squeezed a bit of lime juice on top of it. I know it doesn't sound like much, but it tastes delicious. Properly fermented, the rice is mildly intoxicating and makes people sleepy, but I find it refreshing and energizing.

My life has improved ever since the Midday Meal Scheme was launched in India. They serve a hot, cooked meal at school. Usually, it is dal and rice. In the evening, my mother cooks dinner. At times, it is hot chapattis and a bowl of vegetables, sometimes my favourite, cauliflower and peas. At other times, it is dal and rice. At least now I do not have to sleep on an empty stomach. When Father had left home, I had to do that. I know what it feels like when the stomach growls with hunger, and there is nothing to appease it except glasses of water.

After school, I get ready for the street circus. We move from village to village and perform before the multitudes who throng the street corners. Not everyone pays to watch us perform.

Thankfully, there is no accident while performing the ring of fire this time.

'Why don't you leave the circus?' Ma says. The frown lines on her face have been transformed into deep furrows. It makes her look older than her age. I hope it is sorrow and not anger that has aged her. 'Come and work in Ramu Uncle's ration shop.' She has nothing original to say.

'This is what I love to do,' I murmur. I have no original response either.

'Like father, like son,' she mutters under her breath.

I never talk to my mother about my father. I do not remember him very well. I was four and a half years old when he left home. I am fourteen now, and am the main breadwinner of the family. Of course, the circus does not bring me regular income. It depends on what we earn and the profits are divided among all the artists, and Rahim Chacha, who runs the street circus. He is honest, at least I like to believe so.

Faith moves mountains, doesn't it?

My mother works part-time at Ramu Uncle's ration shop. I see her doling out rice, sugar and kerosene to customers who live below the poverty line. Almost half the village does. She works long hours. Ramu Uncle pays her a pittance, at least I think so. Of course, she brings over leftover food from his house—at times mutton, and if I am really lucky, even chicken.

I am asleep on a Sunday. When I get up, I find my mother clutching a photograph. The photo falls from her hand. I pick it up. She tries to snatch it away from my hand, but I hold on to it. It is the photo which haunts me in my dreams. There are three people in the photograph. I am in the middle, holding a man's hand on the right, and a little fairy's on the left. I frown.

Is it my sister? I peer carefully. No, it must be a fairy.

I have read fairy tales in the school library. She is so tiny. She is barely half my height. I have never seen anyone as small as her.

'Who is she?' I ask Ma. She is reluctant to answer. I wonder why she is so secretive.

'She's your sister,' she says at last.

'Why is she so tiny?'

'She was a midget,' Ma says under her breath. I do not know what a midget is, but am afraid to ask.

'What happened to her?'

'She died,' she says laconically. Mother's voice is indifferent. I would think that she would be devastated.

'Of what?' I persist.

'Pneumonia.'

Pneumonia? I wonder. It is never cold in our village. Not even in winter. We never need to wear sweaters in winter.

'Is that when Father left?' I feel emboldened when I ask this. I have never asked Ma about my father before, perhaps because Ma has never spoken about him. 'It doesn't make sense,' I continue, 'Why did Father abandon us when she was already dead?'

'I don't know,' she says, 'maybe he blamed me for it.' I see the shifty look in her eyes. I realize that she is not telling me the truth. Her litany of complaints against my father continues: 'He deserted us and left me to look after you. Me! With little education and no job. What did he want me to do? How did he expect me to keep the home fires burning? Did he want me to sell myself? Or sell you?' Her tirade continues, but I am happy.

At last, she has begun to talk to me about my father. I remember the tired man who performed in the street circus. It was in his blood, he had said.

The school results are out. I am excited! I have actually passed with flying colours. The circus takes up too much of my time and I had little time to study. But now, I begin to believe in miracles once again. I will now attend the high school in the next village. I bring the report card home. Where is Ma? She is not at home. I am not surprised. I have returned home early. She must still be at the ration shop. I go running to the shop, but it is shut. I see the 'Closed' sign on the door and make a face.

As I turn back, I see that the back door is open. I wish I had not opened the door. I wish I had not seen the tangle of arms and legs on the floor; not seen Ma's saree discarded in a pile, not recognized the gold bangles she wears on her wrist.

I am now on the road again. I have money in my pocket. I have taken it from the sugar tin in the kitchen. Ma thinks I do not know where she hides the money, but I have always known. I have some of my own money as well. I have 500 rupees with me. All this makes me feel rich.

My mind is in a whirl. I have forgotten about the evening show, the ring of fire and Rahim Chacha. I cannot stay here any more. I wonder if this is the real reason my father left the house. I can be anywhere, except in the village. The only place I can think of going to is the city. I see the bus and board it.

In the city, I see big hoardings announcing the Jumbo Circus. I am breathless with excitement. Maybe I can get a job there. I cannot go back home.

Outside the circus, I see a queue. I stand behind and await my turn to purchase a ticket. The show is about to begin. It is not a big circus, but I am enthralled nevertheless. This is how a circus should be. The clowns regale the crowds with laughter. I have never before seen trapeze artists swinging on the trapeze, jumping from one end to the other. Then comes the trampoline, on which a fairy-like girl and a man are performing acrobatics. I see the girl turn cartwheels, and then, like a rubber ball, she bounces up into the air and stands on the man's shoulders. I feel a sense of unreality.

I recognize her as the girl in the photograph.

Ten years have passed, but the girl has not grown at all. She is still the same. I wonder how anyone can remain the same.

Then I remember. She is a midget. Now comes the grand finale. The man, who was with the girl on the trampoline, reappears. Apparently, they are short staffed at the circus. That is why the man performs multiple roles. He comes with a dozen knives. His partner stands on a wooden stand. The man's blindfold is tied tightly across his eyes. His partner stays absolutely still. This is better, much better than what Rahul and Robin do. The entire audience can see the knife-throwing act. He throws the knives with unfailing accuracy. The house breaks into thunderous applause.

I sleep on a railway station bench at night, my money carefully folded and hidden in my socks. The next morning, I return to the circus. The owner is standing outside, chewing betel nut.

'I am looking for a job,' I say, my voice quavering.

'And what can you do?' he asks indulgently.

'Ring of fire,' I say with a confidence I am far from feeling.

'We don't perform it here,' says the circus owner.

'Tightrope walking then,' I say, my face ashen. I hope he does not ask me to demonstrate.

'We are a proper circus, not a street one.' The owner's voice has turned haughty.

I am about to leave when the man, the partner in the knife-throwing act the evening before, comes in.

'I need to go home. My mother has passed away,' he announces.

The owner's displeasure is clear, but he doesn't say anything. Mothers come first, at least in India. The owner knows that his earnings will dip if they do not perform the grand finale. He calls for the knife thrower, beckoning me to stay.

'Satya is on leave for fifteen days,' he says to the man when he arrives. Although Satya has not mentioned the duration of his leave, the owner knows that Satya will not return before performing the tehrvi, the final ceremony, for his mother. The knife thrower's face turns wan.

'But the show must go on,' the owner says. 'I want you to train this boy in place of Satya. It should be no problem.'

The man turns to look at me. I startle.

I must have seen him yesterday but he was so far away. It has been ten years, but the man in the photo is still the same. Things begin to click in my brain. My sister, the midget, and my father. Men must have come to our village when she was small, trying to persuade my parents to sell their daughter. She was an oddity and would be an attraction in a mela or circus. My mother was willing to do so. To her, the little girl brought her disgrace, but my father must have refused, for all the money in the world. Vertically challenged, a dwarf, a midget, whatever she was, she was his daughter. He could not leave her to the wolves, let her be raped, abused and bruised, in any fair or circus. He had walked out with her.

It must have been a difficult choice to make. He had chosen her over me. But I realize he had chosen wisely. Perhaps he had seen Ma with Ramu Uncle, or perhaps that had happened later.

I rush towards him and then stop. What if he doesn't recognize me? He stares at me and continues to stare. I stare back.

'What is the problem?' asks the circus owner. 'You always complain that you have to do all the work, your partner Satya just has to stand still.'

The man, my long-lost father, shoves a photograph towards the owner. It is the same one that Ma had showed me. The one I see in my dreams. 'Father and son,' he says quietly. The circus owner understands.

'My hand may remain steady,' says my father, 'but what if my son moves?'

I want to run and hug my father, but there will be time enough for that. I have waited for so long. I can afford to wait longer. I have all the time in the world to catch up with him. At least, I hope I do.

At night, after the show, we go and sit under a tree, Papa, Ira and I. He offers me parathas and chicken.

'I had hoped that you would do something else with your life,' he says quietly.

Do I hear a tinge of regret in his voice or am I imagining things?

'Why didn't you?' I ask him gently.

'The circus is all I know,' he says.

I nod slowly. 'The circus is all I know too,' I repeat.

Nightmare

I am ready to go. Not just out of this house. I am ready to leave this world as well. A lockdown has been imposed by the prime minister right now, but my life has been in lockdown ever since my husband passed away nearly six months ago.

I know that grief is personal. Most people are resilient. They learn to get on with their lives. However, I lie in bed, staring at the ceiling as if it is the Sistine Chapel at the Vatican. But there are no paintings by Michelangelo on the ceiling.

'Life is ephemeral,' I muse.

'Mom, I want lunch within an hour.'

My son Aniket's voice sounds plaintive. He actually expects me to go into the kitchen and cook a meal for him. I have never stepped into the kitchen before, not once. That isn't true, of course. I have made coffee and tea, boiled eggs and made omelette and noodles. But a full meal? However, these are troubled times. Aniket is working from home and his lunch hour begins at 1.30 p.m.

His timelines are sacrosanct. At least, he pretends that they are.

Pasta, I decide. It is easy to make. I only have to boil macaroni, put it in a sauce—straight out of a jar—and the meal is ready. As a bonus, I decide to make a salad with dollops of mayonnaise in it.

My son looks at the meal stoically. He says nothing. I know what he yearns for: Indian cuisine. Lentils, vegetables, chicken, chapatti and rice. I know that he misses the maid more than I do. The maid would have offered a whole menu to choose from—paneer butter masala, chicken tikka, crisp dosa, dal makhani, dum aloo, chole bhature, puri aloo and chapattis. He had a variety to choose from earlier. Some hope.

I have been a working woman all my life, I retired as a deputy general manager in a nationalized bank, and in India we have always had domestic help. I did not expect the COVID-19 pandemic. Not that anyone did. We did not expect the maids to be banished from our housing complex.

My son looks contemplative. He must be wondering what I will serve for dinner. Maggi noodles and instant soup perhaps? We live on them, and on frozen pizzas.

After lunch, I return to my room and slump in my bed. I shudder at the thought of the dishes I will need to wash. Why didn't Aniket install a dishwasher? Why doesn't he do them? I forget that the cook used to clean the dishes as well.

My thoughts turn towards Pranay. My husband died before COVID-19 hit India. He was there one moment, and gone the next. We were hosting a party at our house in New Delhi and he was standing with a glass of wine, when suddenly, the glass fell from his hand and he dropped to the floor. His friends rushed to him, but he would not move. 'Cardiac arrest,' somebody must have said. An acquaintance started thumping his chest, but nobody could really give him a cardiac massage in time. The ambulance was called, but by the time it arrived, he was no more. 'Brought dead', is what the hospital wrote on his papers. A thirty-five-year-old marriage was over in a moment. COVID-19 struck three months later, while I was still grieving.

My son Aniket was in Mumbai and I was in Delhi when my husband passed away. Aniket promised to rush to Delhi as soon as possible. The very first time he came to Delhi, he saw it all—an empty fridge, a near-empty larder, unwashed clothes piled up in the laundry basket, unwashed dishes in the sink.

'Where is the maid?' he asked.

'She went away for a cataract operation,' I mumbled from my bed.

'For how long will she be away?' he asked.

I did not know. I didn't even recall for how long she had been away already. I had lost track of time. 'You are coming home with me,' he decided. I did not say anything. I had learnt to obey long ago. I accompanied Aniket to Mumbai.

Mumbai was a picturesque city with beautiful beaches and my son tried his best to keep me in good spirits.

He encouraged me to go out for my morning walk, to keep my blood sugar in check.

'Stay healthy, Mom,' he said, 'I don't want to lose you too.'

I began walking around our housing complex, all by myself. Four days later, I saw someone walking by my side. It was my husband, Pranay.

'Tired?' he asked solicitously. 'Sit on the bench and rest.'

I looked at him searchingly and then, sat quietly on the bench, using my scarf to wipe the drops of perspiration from my face. I did not tell Aniket about seeing Pranay. I knew that he would laugh and blame me for my wild imagination. Worse still, he would take me to a doctor and they would subject me to an MRI. The prospect of going into the machine for half an hour, while it wrought havoc with my senses, was something I desperately wanted to avoid.

I knew Pranay was not real. I had gone for Pranay's cremation and I had seen him burn. I had wanted to do that, although women in India rarely attend cremations; I wanted to say my last goodbye to him.

People had imaginary friends. I had a once-real, now imaginary husband to give me company when my son was away at work. I knew that my imagination had created him, but when he was with me, he was real. I knew, or thought I knew, how John Nash felt in the film *A Beautiful Mind*. But the character suffered from schizophrenia. I was merely grief-stricken.

Suddenly, COVID-19 struck India. It caught us unawares. Never, not once in the sixty years of my existence had I experienced something like this.

'Wear a mask,' said Aniket, 'if you ever step out.'

I was embarrassed to do so. 'It is not airborne,' I argued.

'What if it is?' said Aniket. 'No one really knows.'

When the janta curfew was announced on 22nd March people were urged to come to their balconies and clap to show appreciation for the doctors and servicemen who were fighting the pandemic. Aniket coaxed me outside and clapped enthusiastically.

'Will this kill the virus?' I asked sarcastically.

'No.' Aniket was phlegmatic as usual.

'Then what is the point?' I said. 'Plus, we all have to die one day.'

'How philosophical.'

Now Aniket was being sarcastic. His sarcasm was wasted on me.

'Darwin spoke of the survival of the fittest,' I said. 'Let us end the lockdown. Let the fittest survive.'

'Senior citizens, especially those with co-morbidity, are especially vulnerable,' pointed out Aniket, 'and Mom, you have both hypertension and diabetes.'

'I am ready to die,' I insisted.

'Brave words, Mom,' said Aniket.

Life came to a halt after the lockdown. My walks were prohibited. I was confined to the house. The maids I had taken for granted stopped coming. I had not realized how slovenly I had become. There were orange peels on the floor, peanut shells littered on the side table, and discarded piles of clothes in the bathroom. The house began to look like it had never been clean. I had taken it for granted; the maid cleaning the house every morning, the cook making breakfast, lunch and dinner. It was all done within three hours. I merely had to reheat the dinner after Aniket returned from work.

I wonder how my husband would have reacted to the pandemic and the lockdown. He would have been pacing up and down the apartment. He used to walk seven or eight kilometres every day, to stave off his heart problem.

Aniket coaxed me out the next time the prime minister urged us to light a candle during the lockdown. 'Don't worry, Mom,' said Aniket, as we stood on our balcony, 'there will be a vaccine soon.'

'And pigs will fly.' I laughed. I was not being helpful. Aniket was being kind, but I didn't want kindness. I wanted out. I couldn't imagine spending my life without my husband, mourning his loss.

'Those with low levels of vitamin D are especially vulnerable,' said Aniket, as he urged me to sit in the balcony every day.

A few days later we learnt that fourteen migrant labourers, wanting to return to their home state, Bihar, slept on the railway track at night and an oncoming goods train crushed them to death.

'Can anything be more tragic?' lamented Aniket.

'Why did they sleep on the railway tracks?' I mused.

'Well, they thought that no trains were running. They forgot about the goods train,' explained Aniket.

'What a way to go,' I said out loud, 'to die in one's sleep … all problems gone in an instant.'

Aniket does not have to remind me about dinner. I drag myself into the kitchen, take out the sheekh kebabs and Malabar parathas from the freezer and leave them to thaw as I begin to wash the dishes. I decide to heat a packet of dal bukhara from Kitchens of India as well. Half an hour later, I call Aniket for dinner.

'Thank god for frozen food,' he says laconically, as he begins to eat. I ignore him. After dinner, we sit down to watch NDTV news. It is bleak.

'The lockdown has been extended again,' I say.

'More time to spend with the family,' says my son. We see things through different prisms.

I return to my room after dinner and lie down. I switch on the airconditioner and shiver slightly. As the room turns cold, my thoughts turn morbid. I look at the albums by my side and a deluge of memories engulf me. Of travelling abroad. Of being with Aniket and Pranay in Disneyland, on top of the Empire

State building, at the Lincoln Memorial and the Niagara Falls. They were such happy times. Why was God so cruel? Why did he take Pranay away? When my husband passed away, I thought I would die of a broken heart. But do people actually die of something like that? Or do they die a little every day, until there is nothing left?

I am feeling drowsy. My eyes are heavy with sleep. I yawn. The lockdown will be over soon, I think sleepily. But maybe, with the community spread of COVID-19, chances are that once Aniket goes back to work, he will be infected. If he does, so will I. As I am both hypertensive and diabetic, I am particularly vulnerable. I know that there is a shortage of beds in the COVID wards in the hospitals, and a shortage of ventilators as well. In such a scenario, I am likely to die. The prospect does not upset me at all. Now is as good a time as any to die.

Suddenly, I feel claustrophobic.

I get up and open the door leading to the balcony next to my room. I look down from the twenty-fifth floor for a long time. Everything looks so small. I realize that it is time to bid the world goodbye. Aniket will be devastated, I know. He will blame himself for not recognizing just how severe my depression was. He will realize that I needed medical treatment, but he had ignored it. I know that he will get over it. My feet begin to shake as I stand on the ledge. I try to step back, but I falter, and I find myself plunging from the dizzying heights. I scream.

I open my eyes. I am on the bedroom floor. I must have slept and rolled from the bed in my sleep. I get up gingerly. No broken bones.

It was a nightmare, but one that was so real. I look into the mirror. Is that terror-stricken woman really me? I turn to my left. Pranay is by my side. He looks at me sadly and then walks towards the door. He knows that I do not need him any longer.

COVID-19 is a reality. And Mumbai is the worst affected. I hope that I live on. I hope that, by some miracle, the world finds a vaccine very soon. I look at my husband's photo on the wall.

'Forgive me,' I mouth the words silently, 'but I do not want to go out of this world, not for at least another thirty years.'

I guess I am a survivor after all.

Blood Wins

She heard the sound of gunfire in the distance, but it didn't surprise her. The army would be busy with target practice on the hills, she thought. Then she heard it again—short bursts of gunfire, in rapid succession.

Something had happened, something big.

Ashang's face blanched at the thought. Her heart somersaulted. She hoped that Ngaithing was safe, and more importantly, he was not involved in whatever had happened.

What had happened? An ambush? Or had the army run amok and killed suspects? A neighbour told her the news later. An army convoy had been attacked in Ukhrul. Seventeen jawans had been killed, along with a Major of the Indian Army.

Ashang closed her eyes. She knew that repercussions would follow. It was inevitable.

Although her mind was in turmoil, she continued to work mechanically. She plucked the chicken she was about to cook, cleaned it, and butchered it into chunks. She put a ladleful of oil into a pot and placed it on the wooden fire, which was burning brightly in the middle of the room. She stirred in a handful of whole red chillies and salt, added the chicken and a glass of water and let it simmer. It would cook for half an hour, or more, until it was done.

She had begun to feel hungry. She had eaten her first meal hours ago. She looked at her watch and smiled. It was not yet 6 p.m. Night fell quickly in Ukhrul. By 5 p.m. it was dark. She had learnt to sleep by 6.30 p.m.

She lit the kerosene lamp and sat on the stringed cot in the corner of the room, shivering slightly.

Late that night, there was a knock on the door. Her son, Ngaithing, stood outside.

'I need a place to stay for the night,' he said, his face sullen.

She stared at him, stone-faced. A year ago, he had stolen all her jewellery and disappeared from the village. Now, he was back. For a moment, she thought of shutting the door on his face, but she could not do so. After all, he was her blood.

He pushed the door open and entered the house. He did not say anything. He did not need to. His face said it all. He looked tired, very tired. He would have to be—killing seventeen soldiers was tiring, she thought bitterly, although she knew that he had not been working alone. Why was he here? Was he afraid that the army would raid his hideout and flush the insurgents out? There was no point in asking him that. She knew that he would retreat behind a wall of silence. She served him chicken. She also placed some iromba, the pungent concoction of dried fish, bamboo shoots, chillies and potatoes, which he loved, along with some leftover rice. She saw him eating ravenously, and her heart went out to him.

How had he lived this past year? Had he gotten enough to eat? What had spurred him to join the insurgent movement? There were so many questions she wanted to ask. But she knew that every question of hers would be met with stony silence.

A little later, he disappeared into the inky darkness while she wondered if she would ever see him again.

For days, there was silence ringing through the village. She realized that a storm was brewing. Two weeks later, the district administration imposed punitive fines upon the village, for the first time in years.

In 1982, families which paid just 8 rupees as hill house tax, found it impossible to pay punitive fines of ₹200. She waited, heart in mouth, as she saw the district administration take away her brass utensils, her big pots and pans, her goats and her chicken, in lieu of the punitive fines. She was left with almost nothing but the earthen pots.

But it was still not over. A week later, the army went on a rampage.

She could hear the cries of women who were pulled out of their homes. She was not spared either. When she was pulled out of her house, she was shivering. She knew what would follow. She closed her eyes and waited.

Molestation. Rape.

She had heard horrendous stories about it. The Armed Forces Special Powers Act was in force in Manipur and the army was all-powerful. But nothing happened. When she was taken to the army headquarters for interrogation, she began to feel the hunger pangs. She had eaten her last meal the night before. Rice, laisaag or mustard leaves boiled in salted water, a boiled egg and some fish. But it was noon now. She grabbed the bun the officers offered and ate it hungrily. But she could not give them the information that they wanted. She insisted that she did not know where Ngaithing was. She had not seen him since he had left home a year ago.

'He must be in touch with you,' rasped the Colonel. 'Insurgents always manage to stay in touch.'

'How can he,' she asked, 'if, as you say, he has gone underground?'

The Colonel laughed. 'People who go underground still keep in touch with their families,' he said knowingly. She kept silent.

'We will catch him, sooner or later,' he threatened. She still said nothing. The Colonel swore under his breath. She was lying, of course, but he was helpless. He had no choice but to let her go. She returned home grim-faced. She now began to feel concerned about Ngaithing's safety.

She closed her eyes and thought of the time when the hills had resounded with the sound of music and laughter, when guns never boomed, when bloodied and bullet-ridden bodies were not found in the morgue. But life had taken a different turn. Boys, fresh out of school, had become insurgents, and the church, a haven for troubled souls, had become a breeding ground for insurgency. Boys, just half men, bandied about words like 'neocolonialism' and 'imperialism' with ease, waving pamphlets which talked of a utopia, where society was self-sufficient, where communities grew rice, where women wove phaneks and shawls, and men fished in ponds or pokhris. Where was the young boy with sparkling eyes whom she so loved? Where did he disappear? When had he been transformed into a silent man with a maniacal gleam in his eyes, whose hands were now stained with blood?

She entered her house and sat on the stringed cot, her shoulders hunched.

The interrogation was over and her freedom had been but a reprieve, but she knew that this would not last long. The army would keep a watch on her house and interrogate her again and again, in the vain hope that she would reveal Ngaithing's whereabouts. She wished that she could inform him to keep away from the house.

Suddenly, her eyes were drawn to a bundle in the corner of the room. The new phanek she had been weaving was lying on the ground. She grimaced. It would get dirty if left lying there. When had it fallen onto the ground? She was about to get up to pick it when she remembered that she had folded it and placed it near the loom before she had gone out.

Her eyes widened when she saw the bundle move.

Suddenly, Ngaithing was standing before her, wearing the phanek and her new blouse. He was clean-shaven. His lank black hair fell upon his shoulders. She had never realized just how much he resembled her. He picked up a red and black Naga shawl with a thin green strip running around the border and wrapped it around himself. It was an excellent disguise. In the dark, he could be mistaken for her.

He looked at her implacably.

'You must have told the Colonel about my last visit,' he finally said. 'They must have prised the truth out of you.'

'I didn't say a word,' she said.

'They must have tortured you to get at the truth,' he insisted.

'No, they didn't.' She shook her head vehemently in denial. 'And, in any case, I haven't a clue about your whereabouts.'

'But if you did, you would have told them?' His eyes began to glitter.

'Why would I? You are my blood after all.'

'I am afraid that they will try to keep track of your movements and get me through you,' he muttered.

'Then you mustn't come here ever again,' she retorted.

Slowly, he took out a knife. She didn't move as he placed its edge on her neck. 'Or, I could kill you,' he said, 'and then they will not be able to get at me through you.'

She stood still, not daring to breathe. She knew that he would not hesitate to slit her throat if he thought it was necessary. Blood would spew out, but he would walk away without a backward glance. She closed her eyes, waiting for the knife to pierce her skin.

Instead, she heard the knife clatter on to the floor. The door closed quickly and then, he was gone. Once again, blood won.

Essence of a Woman
~~~~~~~~~~~~~~~~~

The moment the plane began its descent into New Delhi, the knot of fear in my abdomen began to tighten. Even after years of air travel, I had not gotten over my fear of flying. I wished that Trisha had been with me on this trip. She would have held my hand and the fear would have abated. I wished that I had splurged for once and taken Trisha with me to France. After all, Paris was a city made for love.

With Trisha, I would have loved to visit the Louvre. We would have seen the Mona Lisa as well as the Arc De Triomphe, walked past France's Tomb of the Unknown Soldier. Together, we would have cruised down the Seine. We would have seen the Eiffel Tower in new luminescence. Without her, it had just been a wrought iron latticed tower.

It was fortuitous that the line at Immigration at the Indira Gandhi International Airport in New Delhi was not long. I lingered at duty-free for a little while. There was just one thing that I wanted to buy.

'Chanel No. 5, the perfume,' I had said. The salesman pushed a bottle towards me non-committally. I squinted at it.

'Chanel No. 5, *the perfume*,' I repeated. 'This is the perfume *spray*,' I emphasized.

The irritation was clear in my voice. I know that I am quick to anger.

'It's the same thing,' he said, his voice bored. He did not like to be woken up from his snooze. I had never met a more lackadaisical salesman.

'Chanel No. 5,' I repeated, thumbing through my iPhone for a picture of the bottle of the classic perfume, then thrusting it at him. He grunted and got up once again, grumbling under his breath. He searched slowly and finally brought out a bottle.

'12,500 rupees,' he said, a bite in his tone. It cost 3,000 rupees more than the spray. Served me right, his baleful glare seemed to say, for disturbing his nap. I paid for it with my credit card and took a taxi home. On the way, I imagined Trisha's hazel eyes lighting up at the sight of her favourite perfume. She had not asked me for a new one, but I had noticed the empty bottle on the dressing table. Nothing escapes me, as I often say. Trisha had not asked me for one because she was cautious with money. It was something she had learnt from me. After all, I worked in the government. I was not a wealthy chartered accountant like my brother, Jatin. I could not afford to splurge, unlike Jatin, who loved expensive cars and his opulent lifestyle.

I smiled. I wanted to see the wonderment in Trisha's eyes when I gifted her the perfume. She would throw her arms around me in delight. On second thoughts, she wouldn't. She was impulsive, but she knew that I didn't like extravagant gestures.

The taxi sped along which didn't surprise me. The roads were deserted in the early hours of the morning. Somewhere near Taj Man Singh Hotel I saw a black BMW pass me by. It looked just like the one Jatin owned. I smiled wryly. I was being fanciful. All black BMWs looked alike; I knew this.

Jatin and I hadn't met for two years, not since I had seen him making a pass at Trisha and had lambasted him. Of course, Trisha had laughed it off.

'It is just his manner,' she had said, 'he likes to flirt.' Her voice had been indulgent. Perhaps she had a soft corner for him. I turned to look at the car, but it was impossible to see who was driving it.

The taxi dropped me at the door. My fingers lingered on the doorbell for a moment. Then, a tiny smile tugged at my lips. I decided that I would surprise Trisha. After all, she was not expecting me. I was due to arrive the next day. I opened the door with my key and left my suitcase in the drawing room.

I entered the bedroom quietly. The room was redolent with the fragrance of roses and jasmine, iris and musk, lily of the valley and vanilla. The fragrance of Chanel No. 5 was like nothing else. As Trisha was fond of saying, it was a woman's perfume, with the scent of a woman.

A new bottle of Chanel No. 5 had been placed on the bed head. It had been sprayed liberally on to the sheets. I could smell something else. What? I shook my head. It was such a familiar fragrance. I knew it well. Why was the name eluding me?

The name came back to me a minute later: Gucci for men. It was a perfume I used, but sparingly, of course. Trisha was asleep. Her nightie was riding high, exposing her pale thighs. I tried to wake her up, but she wouldn't move. I was afraid. Was she unconscious? I shook her again. Was she in a coma? I could not make out if she was breathing. I rang the taxi driver who had just dropped me home. He couldn't have gone too far, I surmised.

'Could you please return to Shahjahan Road?' I asked, a

plea in my voice. 'It's an emergency.' He returned within five minutes.

I couldn't wait for an ambulance while Trisha's life hung by a thread, so I lifted her in my arms and boarded the taxi, while the driver drove at breakneck speed in order to reach the hospital.

'It's an emergency,' I rasped as I raced towards the lift. I was a man demented. Trisha was wheeled in while I waited outside. A little later, a doctor came upto me. 'Your wife was brought in dead,' he said.

'A cardiac arrest?' I asked, feeling completely dazed. I had been too late in getting her medical aid.

'I ... don't know how to give a cardiac massage,' I lamented.

'She died an unnatural death,' the doctor said tersely. I was bewildered. How could she have died an unnatural death? Murder? Who could have killed her? Or had she committed suicide?

Inspector Shekhawat, who came to the hospital a while later, listened to me sympathetically. Trisha's body could not be released just yet, he said. A post-mortem would have to be conducted.

I returned home in a state of shock. It seemed inconceivable that she had died an unnatural death. I was dismayed to find the police all over the house. They were dusting the place for fingerprints. Our bedroom, the scene of the crime, was out of bounds. I decided to move to the guest house at the India International Centre for a day.

Inspector Shekhawat met me the next day. He looked at me for a moment and then looked away. He told me that the post-mortem report had arrived. Trisha had been killed, smothered.

'She wasn't raped, was she?' I asked, suddenly feeling afraid.

'No,' he said, 'there were no signs of a struggle.'

I felt a moment of relief. Then, he added, 'It appeared to be consensual.' I looked at him uncomprehendingly. What on earth was he talking about? Then, I understood.

'I am so sorry,' he said, 'but we will need a sample of your body fluids. To eliminate suspects,' he added apologetically.

'From a grieving husband I had become a suspect?' I thought bitterly. I suddenly remembered the black BMW I had seen near the Taj Man Singh Hotel. *Jatin.* Had I seen him leaving the scene of the crime? My conviction grew that it had to be him. He must have gifted the perfume to Trisha. He knew that she loved Chanel No. 5. I suspect she had always had a soft corner for him.

The police found Jatin soon enough. He lived in an opulent house, in DLF Phase 1, Gurugram. A DNA test was conducted. The next three weeks were traumatic, for both of us. The DNA test confirmed that the body fluids were his. I wonder why he had not admitted to it straightaway? Was he trying to spare my feelings?

'Foolish of him not to have used protection,' said Inspector Shekhawat, looking pityingly at me, when he came to the house. I looked away. I did not need his sympathy.

'She was on the pill,' I said tonelessly. He placed a commiserating hand on my shoulder. To be betrayed by my wife and my own brother, what could be worse?

After he left, I made myself a drink. Then, I slumped on the sofa in the drawing room. I tried not to think of Trisha lying on the bed, a wanton woman, her nightie riding high, revealing her pale white thighs. I tried not to think of her favourite perfume or the lingering fragrance of Gucci for men.

My favourite perfume. And Jatin's too. But what I couldn't forget were the tell-tale stains on the silken sheets. As I said before, I never miss anything. It did not take a genius to work out what had happened. I had been betrayed by my wife and my brother. Trisha had not been expecting me till the next day so she had made no attempts to remove the evidence of Jatin's visit or their liaison. I didn't realize what I was doing when I put the pillow on her face and smothered her.

I called the taxi driver immediately after, to give myself an alibi of sorts. After all, I had arrived just five minutes before. I knew that the CCTV cameras near the Taj Man Singh Hotel would capture Jatin's car and perhaps his face as well. All the evidence pointed towards him. I hoped that he would be arrested and convicted. According to me, he deserved to die. Of course, he would hire the best criminal lawyer available, they would raise the issue of 'mens rea' or guilty intention.

'Why would Jatin, who was having an illicit liaison with his sister-in-law, want to kill her?' he would argue. Well, perhaps she was forcing him to marry her while he enjoyed his freedom as a bachelor. But that theory appeared to be a little far-fetched. He was an adulterer, but that did not necessarily make him a murderer. On the other hand, I had a much better motive for killing my wife. Inspector Shekhawat was a clever man. He was a persistent man. Sooner or later, he would arrive at the truth. But would he have any proof? I doubted it.

In the meanwhile, I had to be very, very careful.

Coma

It was the aroma of cinnamon and apple wafting through the air that woke me up.

'Apple pie!' I yelled, much in the same manner as Archimedes must have yelled 'Eureka' when he discovered the law of buoyancy, except that I didn't recall his name just then. I didn't even realize that I had said the words aloud. I had no idea what a cataclysmic impact my words would have.

I didn't expect to hear the pie dish fall to the floor, nor the voice of a woman wailing, 'Mohan! Where are you?'

'Why are you trying to bring the house down?' Mohan shouted in turn as he lumbered down the stairs. 'What is the goddamn emergency?'

He saw her sitting outside my room, walked inside and staggered when he saw me wide awake.

'You are awake,' he said, disbelieving.

'That's obvious,' I said, staring at the fat, balding man before me. 'Who am I and where am I?'

'You don't remember?' The woman's face crumpled on hearing me speak.

'Oh my god, Mohan, has he lost his memory?' she cried.

'The doctor had warned us of the possibility, Maya,' he said.

'It happens at times after an accident. The doctor said that it will come back—sooner or later.'

'Call Dr Gandhi right now,' she said, her voice quavering, 'and tell him that he is awake.'

'I will, I will,' he said soothingly, 'but it is Sunday, remember?'

'Was I in a coma?' I demanded, feeling helpless. Who were these people? Were they my parents or my captors? Had I been kidnapped? I looked at my wrists surreptitiously. There were no marks on them. I had not been gagged and bound. These were either my parents or hired actors, paid to play that role.

But if they were really my parents why had they not hugged and kissed me after I had woken up from a coma? Were we such an undemonstrative family? Maybe they were actors enacting a really badly written script. I could not be sure.

One thing was certain. I had been in a coma. But for how long?

'For two months,' said the fat bald man. I was forced to accept him as my father. The woman nodded her head vigorously.

'You had an accident, Jay,' she said.

'Jay?' I raised my eyebrows. 'Short for Jacob? Are we Christians?'

'Jayesh,' she said curtly, 'we are not Christians but Hindus.' There were so many questions I was dying to ask her, but suddenly, I began to feel weak. I fell back on my pillow and began to doze.

I woke up after two hours. 'Mother' appeared at the door a few minutes later.

'Get up, Jay,' she said, 'it is ten o'clock now. I have made an omelette for breakfast, just the way you like it.'

I rose reluctantly from my bed. How did I like my omelette? I couldn't remember.

'Brush your teeth before you have breakfast,' she said, and I ambled into the attached bathroom.

'I would hate to visit the dentist again,' I muttered. Again? When had I visited him the first time? I didn't remember, but I did remember sitting on the dentist's chair, while he used the drilling machine to fill the cavity.

While brushing my teeth, I had a peek at the bathroom mirror. I had a sallow complexion, just like the woman who said she had made an omelette. Maybe we were mother and son after all, or maybe my complexion was sallow because I had been confined to the bed for two months.

I returned to the bed. Mother returned with a tray soon after. On it was an omelette and toast and a small jar of peanut butter.

'Eat quickly, or your omelette and toast will get cold,' she said before leaving the room. I mumbled something inaudible in response. I wolfed down the omelette hungrily. I liked everything in it. Mushrooms, cherry tomatoes, Parmesan cheese, shallots and bell peppers. Kidnappers were unlikely to know my food preferences in such minute detail. 'Definitely my parents,' I muttered to myself.

'You seem to be in a good mood,' she said, smiling just a little when she returned to take away the tray.

I frowned. Was I a surly child? Bad-tempered? Not very likeable? Was that why she was so afraid when I woke up from the coma?

'Why was I in a coma?' I asked her as she was about to

leave. 'Was I ill or did I have an accident?' She looked at me for a long time.

'An accident, a boating accident,' she said at last.

'A boating accident?' I echoed. 'Where exactly are we now?'

'Port Blair.'

The capital of the Andaman and Nicobar Islands, a Union Territory in southern India. I remembered reading about it in a textbook.

'You were in a coma for two months. The city hospital discharged you a month ago. The doctors said that there was nothing more they could do for you, so there was no point in keeping you in the hospital. You could remain in a coma for years. Thank goodness you woke up after just two months.'

Dr Gandhi arrived the next day. He was accompanied by a nurse. 'Sister Jyoti,' Mother introduced her to me. Sister Jyoti had looked after me when I was in a coma. But, of course, I had no recollection of that. Dr Gandhi conducted a cursory physical examination and then pronounced me fit.

'His memory will come back one day,' he said casually in response to my mother's question, 'but no one can predict when that will happen.'

'You can't confine me to the bed,' I said petulantly once the doctor had left. 'The doctor has pronounced me fit. I would like to explore the entire house. Maybe it will trigger my memory.'

Mother reluctantly accompanied me out of my room.

We first walked into the drawing room. I looked around it appreciatively. It was tastefully decorated, which surprised me a little. I did not credit my parents with good taste. With his bold and bluff manner, my father reminded me of a travelling salesman, while with her pinched face and sallow complexion,

Mother looked like what she actually was, a browbeaten housewife. I lounged on the sofa and switched on the television. We had Netflix, I remembered. I recalled watching a show on it before my accident. What was the name of the show? I frowned. Why did the name elude me?

'When will my memory come back?' I wondered out loud, suddenly overtaken by anguish.

Mother took me to her bedroom next. It was as dull as their personalities, which should not have surprised me at all. I had read somewhere that a room reflects the personality of its occupants. Next, she took me to 'Papa's study'. I was surprised when I entered. I thought the last thing he would do was study. I asked her about it and learnt from Mother that the word 'study' was a euphemism. It was actually his office. But there was a bookshelf running across one of the walls. I squinted at the books on display and was disappointed upon reading the titles. There was nothing in there that I wanted to read. No whodunits. No science fiction. No Roald Dahl, Hardy Boys or Ruskin Bond. There were a lot of Mills & Boons novels though. Did someone in the family read mushy romances? Did Mother? The thought made me laugh. Was I a voracious reader? Somehow, I doubted it. I certainly did not like romance. The books were well thumbed. Someone in our house was a voracious reader. Mother? Father? Both did not look like they read any fiction.

Then, I began to wonder. How did I know Roald Dahl and Ruskin Bond? Was my memory coming back? I began to experience a kind of dread. Sometimes not knowing was better than knowing. I turned and looked at my mother. Her face was pale. There was a pained look in her eyes. I began to shiver a little.

She shifted, suddenly concerned.

'You are shivering, Jay,' she said, her voice firm. 'You are overstraining yourself. Come back.' I meekly followed her. I was suffering from an information overload. I needed to process all the information I had gathered.

The next morning, Mother took me to see the rest of the house. We went into the guest bedroom. I plonked myself on the double bed. It was definitely softer than mine.

'This bed is softer than mine.' I was petulant.

'You have an orthopaedic bed,' Mother said sternly. 'The doctors insisted that we buy it, as you were likely to be in a coma for a long time. If you notice, so far you have been lying in a hospital bed, which can be raised or lowered.'

I shifted on the bed.

'The bed cost us a lot of money,' she added under her breath, but I heard her.

They should be happy that I am alive,' I thought angrily, *'instead of holding the cost of a hospital bed against me.'* Were they really my parents? I began to wonder once again.

As Mother began to leave, I stopped her. 'There is another room at the back of the house,' I said curiously.

'That room always remains locked,' she said firmly. I expected her to explain but she fell silent. She must have realized that she had only succeeded in piquing my curiosity.

A little later, Mother appeared in my bedroom.

'Lunch, Jay?' she asked in a falsely cheerful manner, akin to what nurses adopt when they attend to patients. I was afraid that she would now say, 'And how are we today?' That is how the nurse had spoken to me when I had undergone my tonsillectomy operation. How did I remember that? So small fragments of my memory were coming back to me, but substantial things were still elusive. Was my memory playing tricks on me?

'Coming,' I said to her.

The next morning, I woke abruptly. Sunlight had begun to stream into the room. I looked out of the window and saw the blue curtains in the neighbour's drawing room fluttering in the breeze. Where was Carbon? She was nowhere to be seen.

How did I remember Carbon, my neighbour's Siamese cat? Maybe my memory had really started to come back. Maybe I would remember the woman with the pale lips and sallow complexion who, I was told was my mother. And the bald, fat man who I had begun addressing as Papa.

A little later Carbon came to the lawn for a leisurely stroll. Suddenly, a little black dog appeared from nowhere and began to chase after her. I knew the dog. I remembered that I had tied a cracker on his tail and had lit it with a match. Frightened by the crackling, it had yelped. I remember that I had clapped my hands and laughed. Luckily, the dog had not been hurt. I was grounded for a week by my father. 'Why is he like this?' he had muttered. 'What did we do to deserve him?' I was not very likeable, I surmised, remembering the incident.

The persistent ring of the landline made me leave the bed. Mother went to the drawing room hurriedly to answer it.

'I can't come,' I heard her say. 'Jay has just come out of coma, you know …' Silence. 'Oh, your hip is fractured,' she said. Then, a minute later, 'That is really awful. Has somebody called for an ambulance? I'll come. Yes, yes. That's what friends are for.'

I heard her enter my room before I saw her. Her face was tense. 'Mrs Das,' she began saying.

'Carbon's owner?' I asked. Her eyes narrowed.

'How do you know Carbon? Has your memory returned?' she asked suspiciously.

'No,' I said, 'I just recall the cat's name and the fact that I had my tonsils out.'

She looked searchingly at me and finally said, 'I have to rush. I will have to take Mrs Das to the hospital. Have some muesli with cold milk for breakfast. Make a tomato sandwich for yourself for lunch, just in case I do not return in time. I have left everything you need on the kitchen counter. I am locking the door from outside. If you wander off, you may get lost.' With that she locked the door and left.

I went into the kitchen and opened the packet of muesli, filled half a bowl with it, and then poured some cold milk on top. It was not as good as the omelette, or the pancake, or the potato paratha which she had been feeding me, but it would have to do.

Then I marched towards the locked room. My curiosity was aroused and I now had an opportunity. I wondered what was inside. I closed my eyes and let my imagination wander.

My favourite fantasy was that of Bluebeard, of course. I had read somewhere that he chopped off the heads of all his wives and threw them inside a room. I wondered how many heads were inside the locked room. Four, maybe five? *'Has Ma ever peeped inside?'* I wondered, laughing to myself. No wonder she appeared to be so scared. She was afraid of Papa. Perhaps she didn't know for sure. Not knowing is worse than knowing. At least the truth cannot kill us all.

Perhaps it can.

'Maybe there was no Bluebeard,' I said to myself, abandoning that fantasy. Perhaps it was the shrivelled mother from the film

Psycho. That was the film I was watching on Netflix before my accident. The one who committed all the murders inside the Bates Motel. But I was wrong. It wasn't the mother but Norman Bates who was the real killer. If my grandmother's skeleton was inside the locked room, it would make Papa a Norman Bates.

'God!' I laughed.

I had a morbid imagination for a fourteen-year-old. How did I remember that I was fourteen? Did Ma tell me? Or was it another fragment of memory which had come to me, another missing piece in the jigsaw?

Perhaps the room at the back of the house was just a storeroom. Maybe it contained junk, things I knew nothing about.

'Curiosity killed the cat,' I said to myself.

'Let sleeping dogs lie,' I reminded myself.

Why were these proverbs tormenting me now, I wondered, just when I was trying to assuage my curiosity? I stood outside the room, torn between caution and curiosity.

Finally, curiosity won.

I walked confidently into my parents' room and rifled through Ma's dressing table. After a few minutes, I found what I was looking for. A hairpin. I straightened it and went towards the room. I jiggled the lever for some time and heard a click. I wondered how I had known to open locked doors.

I recalled something I had read. It said that although a person may suffer from amnesia, he does not forget the skills he possesses. Evidently, I had not forgotten mine.

The door opened noiselessly. The room was spotless. It was evident that someone dusted and cleaned the room every day. Then, I saw the photo on the wall. My sister. Sheela. It did not take me even a minute to recognize her. Suddenly, everything came back to me in a flash: our frequent fights, my being punished regularly for troubling her, our going for a boat ride at our parents' suggestion, in the forlorn hope that we would bond together if we were alone.

If my parents had not discriminated between us, not made it clear that they preferred their picture-perfect daughter over their delinquent son, I would not have begun to trouble her. Left alone in the boat with her, I began to tease her, pinching her at times, pulling her hair, doing everything a naughty, troublesome child would do. Sheela was rowing the boat. Suddenly, she turned towards me in a demonic rage. I wonder if Sheela's anger was spontaneous, or if she had planned this.

'You pest, you dog, you viper. Ever since you were born you have ruined my happiness. How I wish you were dead.'

I was shocked and speechless. My parents expected me to say these things; they would never have expected Sheela to speak in this manner. Suddenly, she gave me a mighty shove and I lost my balance. She meant to throw me off the boat.

I tried to hold on to the boat with all my might, but she swung the oar and hit me on my head. The boat lurched just then and she too fell into the water, just when I lost hold of the boat and began to drown. I don't know how I survived. I can't swim very well. Perhaps I left my body free and began to float. The next thing I remember is waking up from the coma. Sheela must have plunged into the water and hit her head on the corals. I really don't know what happened to her.

'I lost my daughter,' I heard Ma shout that night, when my parents thought I was fast asleep.

'I know, Maya,' Papa said. 'I am sure it was an accident.

Do you think a fourteen-year-old boy could fake everything, the drowning as well as the memory loss? Do you think he is capable of killing his sister? It must have been an accident.'

'She was the sweetest and gentlest of creatures. I mourn her death every day. Sometimes, I wish …'

She left the sentence incomplete, but I knew what she was about to say. My mother wished that I had died instead of Sheela. 'We will know the truth, once his memory comes back,' Papa said.

'If only I knew,' sobbed Mother, 'if only I knew the truth.'

'Shh … stop crying. One day his memory will return and he will remember everything.'

My memory has returned. I remember everything. Sheela pushing me off the boat, hitting my head with an oar, the boat lurching and Sheela falling off the boat, just before I lost consciousness. I realize now why the smile never reaches Ma's eyes. My parents had made their daughter's room into a relic. They love their daughter. They look at me and wonder. They want to know the truth.

But I wonder if I can tell them the truth and shatter their illusion. Will they believe me if I do? I doubt it. Will it be better to pretend that the memory of the accident was erased from my mind and let the truth remain buried forever? I really don't know.

Hell Hath No Fury

I love to travel by air but I am rather ambivalent about taking train journeys. I dislike railway platforms, the intransigent coolies and the jam-packed railway compartments. Train journeys have their advantages. They allow me to meet a number of people. People fascinate me. I love to study human behaviour. I am an amateur psychologist.

But still, I prefer peace and quiet.

As I entered the compartment I was in a reflective mood. I prayed that I would be alone in the air-conditioned first class coupe. I was disconcerted when I found a man already sitting there. He had the flamboyant good looks of a film star or a well-known model. Beside him sat a woman. She was tall and willowy, with shoulder length hair and a beautifully chiselled face. I gasped inaudibly. I have seldom seen someone so beautiful.

The man looked at me and grimaced. I am sure it was nothing personal. I guessed that he too had been hoping for solitude. I glanced at the luggage placed below his seat and read his name: Akshay Kamra.

The name meant nothing to me, but at least I became sure of one thing. He was definitely not a film star. The lady, whose name I did not know, was carrying a Louis Vuitton bag. The couple reeked of money.

Just before the train began to move, yet another passenger entered the compartment. With his silver grey air and extremely fair complexion, he reminded me of Richard Gere in *Pretty Woman*. He carried with him a large suitcase, a strolley and a wicker basket. Compared to him, I was a hitchhiker. I merely had a backpack.

'How much luggage did one need for a day trip to Agra?' I wondered. But of course, I had no idea how long his trip would be.

'Hello,' he said as he slumped into his seat.

Akshay Kamra's face became petulant. He chewed at his lower lip. He probably considered one co-traveller an intrusion; two were definitely a crowd. He pulled out a book from his bag and began reading it intently. He could not have made it more obvious that he resented the intrusion.

The new occupant ignored him. He seemed self-absorbed. Apparently, his strategy worked. Being ignored always piques the interest of the other party. Akshay Kamra looked intrigued. The newcomer suddenly seemed uncomfortable. The reason for his discomfiture soon became evident, as we heard movements inside the wicker basket. It was clear that the wicker basket contained an animal. The man turned towards us apologetically.

'I am sorry,' he said. Then he unfastened the wicker basket. 'This is Snowy, my Pomeranian,' he said. 'I was informed that pets are allowed only in the first class compartment, that is why I had to book this seat.'

A little white head peeped out of the wicker basket.

'Snowy has her muzzle on,' he added, to allay our fears. I

shrank back a little. I was afraid of dogs—be they Alsatians, Labradors or Pomeranians. Surprisingly, Akshay's face lit up.

'I love dogs,' he said, enthusiasm creeping into his voice. 'Sharda loved them too.'

'Sharda?' The stranger looked at him curiously.

It seemed obvious that the lady with Akshay was not Sharda. She shrank away from the dog, as though it was a rabid Rottweiler and not a Pomeranian. Snowy growled. Could dogs smell fear? I wondered. Clearly, Snowy did.

'Who is Sharda?' the stranger asked, more out of politeness than curiosity.

'She was ...' Akshay hesitated for a moment, then said 'my wife.'

'Oh.'

I began to look at the lady sitting beside Akshay with curiosity.

'This is Aarti,' said Akshay, turning his head towards her, 'my wife.'

'Oh!' said the stranger again. Both he and I were curious, although we tried our best not to show it.

The silence grew. Snowy jumped out of the wicker basket and jumped on to Akshay's lap as though she was meeting a long-lost friend, and Akshay began to stroke her fur gently. The train picked up speed. Snowy began to lick Akshay's hands, her red tongue darting in and out. Soon, she had moved towards his face. I thought he would explode in anger, but he merely cuddled Snowy in his arms. He genuinely loved dogs.

'I am Arun Kumar, Senior Marketing Manager, Godrej,' said the stranger, introducing himself, now that the ice had been broken.

'Amitabh Khare, Computer System Analyst,' I mumbled.

'Akshay Kamra,' said Akshay somewhat brusquely.

'Akshay Kamra. Now where have I heard the name before?' said Arun Kumar, wrinkling his forehead.

'I don't know.' Akshay shrugged, 'I am certain we have never met.'

'CMD of Kamra Industries ...' said Arun Kumar slowly, 'whose wife committed suicide sometime ago.' His voice petered off as he realized the gaffe he had just committed.

Akshay smiled mirthlessly. 'Who was arrested by the police for abetment to suicide and was let off for lack of evidence.'

'I am *so* sorry,' stammered Arun Kumar. 'I didn't mean to offend you.'

'No offense taken,' cut in Akshay, 'The police were quite right. I was responsible for her suicide.'

Silence followed his pronouncement. Aarti appeared to be completely mortified by Akshay's bald statement; we were, after all, strangers. Only Akshay seemed to be enjoying the tableau he had created.

'I am sorry, I know very little about the case, only what I read about it in the newspapers, and that was sometime ago,' said Arun Kumar apologetically. I continued to remain silent.

'Two years, one month and fifteen days,' said Akshay.

Aarti turned towards him, surprised. It seemed that she had not realized that Akshay had been counting the days since Sharda's suicide.

'See,' Akshay said, opening his iPhone and showing Sharda's photo to Arun Kumar, 'this was my Sharda.'

Arun did not see it, but I saw Aarti flinch. I lowered my eyes in compassion. I could gauge Aarti's humiliation. She was married to a man who still pined for his first wife. How painful it must be, and how humiliating for her. I felt a flash of anger towards him. Two years was sufficient to get over the loss of his wife and to try to build a new life with his present wife, I thought a trifle sanctimoniously, although frankly speaking, I had no means of knowing. I am a bachelor. Aarti must have thought that her love and patience would win Akshay over, that is, in the course of time. Perhaps she now realized that to him she was merely a convenience.

Arun Kumar glanced at Sharda's photo and could not hide his surprise.

I could not help glancing at the photo too, and I realized why he was surprised. Sharda appeared to be a simple, rather plain-looking girl. She was short with a round face, brown eyes and hair that fell till her waist. There was nothing spectacular about her. I looked at Aarti and wondered if Akshay Kamra was blind. But there was no accounting for taste and perhaps to Akshay, Sharda was perfection personified.

'Sharda was a nursery school teacher. I met her at a school function where I was the chief guest,' he said, his voice dreamy. 'She escorted me during the function. It was love at first sight for me. I had never felt anything like that before. She was so shy and vulnerable. I broke off my engagement to Aarti.' He looked at Aarti apologetically.

'Aarti understood. She realized how I felt. After all, we had grown up together. Sharda and I were married within a month.'

'And the rest, as they say, is history,' Aarti said with a small, brittle laugh. Akshay turned to look at Aarti. He appeared to be surprised. It was almost as if he had never heard her speak sardonically before. Arun Kumar now looked expectantly at

Akshay, as if silently urging him to get along with his story.

'Aarti and I are going to Agra by train,' said Akshay, 'because that is how Sharda and I had travelled. Sharda had never travelled by air. She probably had a fear of flying, and she suffered from carsickness as well.'

'While I have neither,' interrupted Aarti in a rather high-pitched voice, 'I wanted to fly to Agra.'

Akshay seemed not to have heard Aarti, but I did.

'Though she had lived in Delhi all her life, she had never seen the Taj Mahal; she wanted to see this "symbol of love" with her husband. That was my Sharda, a child made for love.'

'It is not a symbol of love,' said Aarti sarcastically, 'it is a mausoleum.'

Akshay's face turned white. I wondered what lay beneath the façade of their seemingly normal marriage.

For a moment, Akshay was quiet. Then he continued, as though there had been no interruption.

'It was Valentine's Day. I had been away in London for a meeting …'

Akshay had a dreamy look as he continued, pulling us into his tale.

'But I made sure that I returned in time to be with Sharda. She was delighted to see me. She flung her arms around me and kissed me. That evening, as we were getting ready to go out for dinner, she said she had something to tell me.

'I wondered about it. Just then, the doorbell rang. The maid had gone out, Sharda was getting dressed, so I opened the door. A courier stood at the doorstep with a parcel for Sharda, which was unusual. I opened the parcel without a thought and saw a sheer black dress. I wasn't sure if it was a dress or negligee.

There was something very intimate about the gift. A message accompanied the gift. It said, "Happy Valentine's Day, my love".

'Of course, I shook Sharda like a ragdoll. I was a man demented by jealousy. Sharda was trembling. She had never seen me so angry.

'I do not know who sent it, Akshay,' she had stuttered.

'Do you have so many lovers that you do not know who sent it?' I had hissed.

She shook her head. "You know that's not true," she said.

'Wear it,' I had commanded. She had mutinously refused.

'Wear it,' I remember thundering. So she walked into the bathroom, her shoulders bowed and returned a little later, the little black dress extenuating her voluptuous curves. She was crying. Whoever had sent it knew her very well. I had never seen her look so lovely before.

'Suddenly I wanted to throw up. I rushed into the bathroom and began to retch. Then, I began to weep. Sharda began to bang at the door. When at last I was exhausted I came out and found Sharda standing outside. I pushed her aside, went to the bedroom and started packing my suitcase. "I am checking into a hotel," I said, "I want you out of the house by the time I return home tomorrow."

'You can't throw me out of the house like this,' said Sharda, tears streaming down her face, 'I am your wife, dammit, and the mother of your unborn child.' I realized that this was the news she had wanted to give me.

'I don't know who the father of your child is,' I had told her callously, 'and frankly, I don't want to know either. I don't want to see you again.'

'I left the house without turning to look at her stricken

face, climbed into my car and left. I checked into the Leela Palace Hotel for the night and returned to my house in Greater Kailash the next afternoon. On my return, I rang the doorbell. The maid, who opened the door, looked worried. She informed me that memsaab had not come out of the bedroom since the morning. I began to panic. I pushed the door with all my might but the door did not budge. I called for the driver ... and together, we broke open the door.

'I remember it like it was yesterday. Sharda was lying in bed, her face peaceful in repose. My anger had abated by then. I had had time to think things over. Once time had passed, I felt that I should have listened to her side of the story. I knew in my heart that Sharda would never betray me ... I touched her hand ... It was cold. I did not need a doctor to tell me that Sharda was dead. So, yes. I can never forgive myself.'

A silence stilled the compartment.

'Maybe ... she killed herself out of guilt.' Arun Kumar spoke finally, consoling him.

'Or maybe someone so jealous of my happiness did this to ruin us,' Akshay spoke bitterly. 'After all, if she'd had a lover, she would have gone to him instead of taking her own life.'

He glanced affectionately towards his current wife. 'Aarti has been such a brick,' he said. 'But for her I would have lost my sanity. She did not hold a grudge against me for breaking off our engagement and stepped back into my life when Sharda left. But I still do not know who could hate Sharda and me so much.'

The atmosphere inside had become claustrophobic, although we were in a first class coupe. Aarti left the coupe to go to the washroom, and I too left it soon after, excusing myself saying that I had to stretch my legs. Aarti came out of the washroom after some time, her eyes glistening with tears.

'Who knew it would end this way?' she said, to me, grabbing my attention with her intent gaze. 'When I had sent the parcel to Sharda, all I had wanted to do was cause a rift between them. I wanted Akshay to divorce Sharda. I wanted to reclaim the place which had been mine since childhood. Akshay may believe that we were merely good friends, but I was besotted with him. I thought I had played a masterstroke. I knew that their marriage would end in a divorce ... I did not realize that Sharda, that simple, unsophisticated girl, would hold Akshay's heartstrings so tight ... that Akshay would still be unable to forget her.

'I had no idea that she was about to bear Akshay's child. I did not realize that he would never see me as anything but a good friend. Sharda's ghost will continue to haunt me all my life and it will not let me rest.'

I stared silently at Aarti. Horror grew on my face. It was not merely her confession that terrified me. It was Akshay Kamra, standing outside the coupe, listening to every word she was saying.

The Quest

I love Mount Abu, and not only because it is my home—even if it is temporary. I love everything about it. I love the Aravalli mountains that surround the town, the cool air that blows across the Nakki lake and calms my senses and the Dilwara temples, whose white marble and exquisite craftsmanship holds me spellbound whenever I visit. But what I love most is the profound sense of peace I experience when I visit the Brahma Kumari Ashram in Mount Abu. I merely have to close my eyes and the ghosts that torment me all disappear. I feel as though I have been granted parole from the prison in which I have been serving a life sentence.

The truth is that I am in Mount Abu to find myself. Somewhere in the journey of my life, I had lost myself.

I need to find my way back.

I know what it is that ails me. It is guilt. I cannot help but remember the day it all began. It began at a birthday party in New Delhi, three years ago. I remember the party so well. It was one of those parties which go on and on, which one attends for all the wrong reasons, where jaws ache from smiling all the time, where it would be considered rude to stalk off midway; where, after some time, the smell of stale beer and roasted peanuts envelops everyone, and the curtain of smoke makes one long for a breath of fresh air.

I had fled from the atmosphere to a small bench in the garden and gulped the fresh air. 'Thank God,' I muttered to myself, 'another five minutes and I would have suffocated and died.'

Then, suddenly, I heard deep-throated laughter, camouflaged as a cough. I noticed a shadow at the end of the bench. I got up to leave, feeling, quite unreasonably, that my privacy had been invaded, although the man had been sitting there before I had joined him. But I sat down once again. There was something about the night, a strange calm, a stillness, a new configuration of stars which, it seemed, would change my destiny.

We sat in silence, antagonistic at first, then neutral and, finally, friendly.

'What are you trying to escape from?' he asked.

'Nothing.'

'If that were the truth, you would be inside the house singing "Happy Birthday" like the rest of the guests,' he said cynically, 'not sitting in the semi-darkness with a man you don't even know.'

'Nor do I care to,' I retorted, stung to the quick. 'I can be alone in a crowd, I have learnt that art.'

He laughed that deep-throated laugh once again. '*So,*' he persisted, 'what are you escaping from?'

I smiled in spite of myself.

'Marriage.'

'Why?'

Somehow, his words were not an intrusion. It seemed like he genuinely wanted to know.

'I do not like the idea of being paraded like cattle in a fair,' I muttered. He turned to look at me, screwed up his eyes, and caught the moonlight on my face. 'If you were indeed cattle in a cattle fair,' he said solemnly, 'I suspect you could fetch a fair price.'

I laughed aloud.

'There is some other reason for your fear, isn't it?' he hazarded.

I turned away, not willing to open up to a veritable stranger and yet, not able to remain silent.

'Your parents' unhappy marriage?' he guessed. I was quick to rebut the suggestion.

'They had the happiest marriage on earth.'

And indeed, they had, if happiness was gauged by the number of fights a couple had. I knew that I was being unfair to my parents. I was aware of the quiet affection that existed between them. I had seen my father massage my mother's leg whenever she had a muscle cramp. I had seen Ma wait till midnight for my father to return home before she served herself some dinner.

'Then what is it?' the stranger persisted.

I swallowed. I thought of the two vitiligo marks on Rati's back, which Rati could never see but they had cast a blight on her life.

'My sister has vitiligo,' I said, my words stark, falling like grains of salt on open wounds, 'and her life has been made hell because of it.'

He looked at me with sudden understanding and although it was dark, it seemed that he could see the pain, the humiliation and the hurt Rati had suffered, simply because four inches of melanin had disappeared from her body.

'Papa had told Rohit's father about Rati's vitiligo,' I said, 'and they decided to overlook it, in exchange for two lakh. But that did not end the torture. Rati has been very sensitive, ever since the patch was discovered. My parents did everything to help Rati. But they felt that they had somehow let their daughter down.'

'I have seen Rati shrivel up before my own eyes. I have seen a happy and outgoing girl transformed into an introvert. Then, of course, the patch grew.' I broke off, unable to continue.

The stranger kept silent, appreciating my need for privacy.

After a while, I continued, 'Rohit came home one day and deposited her back. I remember what he said. "I am sorry." He was unable to meet my parents' eyes. "I cannot live with someone who looks more and more like a chessboard every day." This, when the patch was not even visible to an outsider,' I raged, then quietened. 'But the fear that it would grow and cover her face and neck must have tormented him. I saw something die within Rati that day. I saw her diminished. She didn't rave or rant. Nor did she plead or beg. She remained silent. Since then, she has turned into a recluse.'

'But having vitiligo does not make someone a criminal.' He looked at me in surprise. 'It is treatable, people are using stem cells from the placenta to regenerate the melanin in the skin. Why don't you have Rati treated?'

'Oh, we will,' I said, 'and who knows, Rati's vitiligo may be cured, but who will heal Rati?' I could still see Rati's face crumple on hearing Rohit's cruel jibes. Nobody knew how Rati must have felt when the man who had been making love to her for months could not see beyond the layers of epidermis and dermis.

'I can understand your rage against your brother-in-law, and I appreciate your concern for your sister,' the stranger said, 'but I don't think you have anything to fear. Just because your sister has vitiligo doesn't mean that you will have it too.'

'We are just two sisters, and right now, my parents need both of us,' I said evasively.

That wasn't true. Sometimes things are destined, like my meeting Dilip so unexpectedly; like our growing friendship and his proposal of marriage. The phrase 'swept off my feet' did not mean anything to me until Dilip swept me off mine.

My father opposed the marriage, he felt that something was wrong. There was nothing he could pinpoint except this feeling that he had in his gut. Perhaps he had become more perceptive, or perhaps merely more apprehensive. Since Papa had nothing but his gut feeling to go on, I paid no heed to him. Women in love seldom heed others, not even their parents. But I had so much more to go on.

The speculative gleam in Dilip's eyes, for instance, when he casually lifted my phone and scrolled down the list of phone calls I had made, or the list of emails. When did his love turn into an obsession? I had no idea but it scared me.

'You remind me of Nana Patekar in *Agnisakshi*,' I told him, but he was not deterred by the comparison.

'It took you one hour and twenty minutes to reach home,' he said gratingly one day, 'it normally takes you twenty minutes.'

'I sat in the coffee house and had a cup of coffee,' I explained.

The truth was that I had begun to feel caged in the house. I cherished these moments of freedom.

'Alone?' Dilip's voice had become sharp.

'Of course, alone,' I retorted.

He slapped me hard. 'Liar,' he screamed, 'who were you with?'

I did not know what upset me more, the searing slap or Dilip's face, contorted with rage, which seemed to belie his protestations that he loved me. I did not wait to hear another word. I returned to my room, shoved some clothes into my strolley bag and readied to leave.

'Anu,' said Dilip, his voice low, 'where are you going?'

'I am leaving,' I said. 'I am returning to my parents' house. I will allow no man to hit me.' Saying this, I strode out of the house.

Dilip shouted at me, a plaintive note in his voice, 'Anu, wait—just wait—don't go.'

But I wouldn't let Dilip stop me. I raced out of the house.

Perhaps Dilip had tried to follow me. Perhaps he had given up before he had even started. Perhaps he thought he could wait for my anger to blow over. It was lucky that I was able to hail a passing cab immediately after leaving the house. I took a flight to Jaipur. If Papa and Ma were surprised to see me, they said nothing. Perhaps this was what they had feared the most, a daughter standing outside the door, like unclaimed goods duly returned to the sender. But I was no Rati. My eyes blazed with anger even though I said nothing.

Dilip rang home the next day, and spoke to me as though nothing had happened.

'Come home,' he said.

I banged the phone down without responding. Papa looked up from the newspaper he was reading, his eyes questioning. I continued to butter my toast with studied nonchalance. My mobile phone rang an hour later.

'I can't live without you, Anu,' said Dilip, 'please come back.'

'I need time to think,' I responded brusquely.

'Think about what?' he asked.

'Whether I want to continue in this marriage or not.'

'Will you break up our marriage because I hit you once?' he asked.

'How many times do you think you should hit me before I am allowed to call it quits?' I responded.

'I did not mean that—' he stuttered, 'it will never happen again, I swear.'

'I don't trust you any more.'

Then, I switched off the phone.

'What happened?' Ma asked. All this while she had refrained from asking me any questions, not one since I had arrived. I sighed and narrated the entire incident to her.

'Marriage is a series of give and take, Anu,' she said. 'These things happen. You must learn to adjust. Simply because Rati's marriage turned sour does not mean yours will too.'

'Don't mind me.' Rati spoke up suddenly. 'You can always pretend that I don't exist.'

'I didn't mean it like that,' Ma said quickly, surprised, but Rati had already burst into tears. There was a sudden silence in the room. Then Rati got out of her chair, toppling it over, and rushed out of the room. I stood up uncertainly, wondering if I should go after her. Ma shook her head gently. I sat down once again.

'I would rather cut my losses and move on,' I said, 'than live with a violent man.'

'You can't live life your own way all the time,' Ma urged. 'Try to make your marriage work.'

The telephone rang as soon as I woke up the next day. It was Dilip again. His voice sounded slurred.

'Anu, if you don't return home by noon tomorrow, you will find me dead,' he said.

I laughed loudly, a harsh grating laugh which sounded unpleasant even to my own ears.

'Words,' I spat, 'cowards like you only threaten with words. Only cowards hit their wives.' This time, it was Dilip who banged the phone down. I raised my head and saw my mother's shocked face. She had come to give me bed tea.

Dilip rang up again at teatime. This time he was crying.

'Remember what I said, Anu,' he said. 'I can't live without you. If you do not return by noon tomorrow, you will find me dead.'

I sat swirling my tea with a spoon.

'I'm getting you a train ticket for tonight, or a flight ticket if you want,' Papa said after he heard about the incident. 'I want you to go home.'

'No, Papa,' I said. 'We have been married for just three months and he has already hit me. He must learn to not repeat this ever again. I will not become his punching bag.'

'Anu,' my mother's stunned voice intruded into my speech.

'Forget it, Ma,' I said, 'let me live my life my own way.'

'What if it turns out to be true?' Ma asked an hour later. 'Can you live with the sorrow and the guilt? Won't Dilip's face haunt you throughout your life? Will you be able to close your eyes and see anything other than Dilip's tortured eyes? Will you be able to bear the taunts of people who will say, "Her husband is dead because of her"?'

'But he hit me, Ma,' I said, 'and you know violent men never change.'

I saw my mother's knowing eyes and added, 'What do you know about it? Dad has never laid a finger on you.'

Ma kept looking at me unblinkingly. Finally, she sighed and said, 'Your father never touched me, certainly, but you have no idea what he can do.'

She suddenly got up. 'Come with me,' she said, and began walking towards the attic. I followed, knowing that Ma's knees ached as she climbed the stairs slowly, resting after every few steps, till at last, we reached the top. Then, Ma walked towards an old steel trunk and opened it.

My nostrils were assailed with the musty smell of old woollens covered in mothballs. Ma was rummaging inside the trunk. With a gasp, she dug out a bundle of letters wrapped with a pink satin ribbon. I opened it slowly and recognized the handwriting immediately. I smiled a little as my eyes quickly scanned the letters. They were love letters written by my father.

'Dad certainly was not a great writer.' I chuckled under my breath. Dilip's letters to me were definitely far more romantic. 'Dad and you had the perfect marriage,' I said, turning to face Ma, 'so what's new?'

'Look at the address,' Ma's voice sounded strange.

Perplexed, I turned the envelope. Startled, I looked at the address again. 'Malavika Ghosh. Who …? Who … is she?' I could barely recognize the stuttering voice as my own.

'I don't know. I have never asked,' Ma said. 'I found the letters in your father's drawer. Obviously, she had returned them to him once the affair had ended. He made me say sorry,' said Ma sadly, 'for invading his privacy, opening his locked drawer and reading his letters. The affair was over and he never once apologized for cheating on me. He showed no remorse. I stayed with him because of you and Rati ...'

'And because you had nowhere else to go,' I said harshly.

Ma flushed. 'We all live our lives differently. Some compromise because they are in a position of weakness, as I did; I had no choice, you're right. Some compromise from a position of strength, as you well may, because you are large-hearted enough to forgive. Believe me, Anu, physical hurts go away, the other hurts never do.'

I looked at Ma's face as though seeing her for the first time. When had Papa betrayed Ma? I did not recall any ugly scenes and no undercurrents of tension in the house. How had Ma maintained the facade of a happy marriage for so long? I wanted to ask but stopped in time, deciding that I would not strip her of the remnants of her dignity. I wondered what it had cost Ma to tell me about Papa's affair. A lot of courage, I guessed. Nobody wants to confess that their life partner had betrayed them and not even regretted it.

'I will return ... not by the evening train, but the morning train tomorrow. Dilip must learn to wait,' I said.

As I boarded the train the next morning, I heaved a sigh of relief. I even began to look forward to returning home. Dilip was obsessively in love with me, I reminded myself, and he had not been unfaithful. I wondered if I could cope with infidelity. Perhaps not. Of course, we had not been married long enough. But Ma's story made me realize that women have to take a great deal in their stride.

The train reached after noon. I should have known that Indian trains would never be on time. After reaching home, I rang the doorbell but there was no response. By the time I rang it a second time, my anger was about to erupt. I regretted giving in to Ma and returning home. When no one opened the door the third time I rang the bell, I remembered that I was carrying a set of house keys with me, and opened the door.

I surveyed the drawing room soon after I entered. Cobwebs hung on the ceiling and the remnants of breakfast or lunch lay on the table. Coffee dregs floated out of the half-turned cup, the edges of the toasted bread had been littered on the table-top, along with the egg shells. Soggy cornflakes floated in a dish containing cold milk.

'Definitely breakfast, not lunch,' I surmised. I suspected that the maid had taken the day off.

I went to the bedroom and found the door locked. All the other rooms were empty. Where was Dilip? I began to panic. I called my neighbour for help. By now I knew something was seriously wrong. It took my neighbour a great deal of effort to break open the bedroom door. We found Dilip hanging by the ceiling. He had left behind no suicide note.

If only I had not walked out of the house that day. Many wives are beaten, many are battered, yet they continue with their lives as if nothing happened. But I was not able to tolerate even a slap. I was angry and unforgiving and chose to leave. And I did not return home in time.

Dilip died because I was unable to forgive. I blame my anger and pride for what happened. His slap hurt my pride and self-esteem, but more than that, it enraged me. I never took Dilip or his obsessions seriously, I never tried to appreciate his misgivings and understand the monsters that tormented him.

I cannot imagine his last few hours. He loved me obsessively. I could never cope with that kind of love.

The guilt of not returning in time continues to gnaw at

me. My neighbours looked at me with suspicion. Who would believe that Dilip had killed himself because I had reached home two hours late? Every time I close my eyes, I see him hanging from the ceiling. I have been unable to sleep for years.

I sit and pray in the Brahma Kumari Ashram every evening. I hope that I will be able to purge my guilt. Perhaps I was not responsible anyway. Perhaps Dilip would have committed suicide, if not that day, then some other day. Who can know?

But he had his revenge. He left me burdened with a sense of guilt so unassailable that I have not been able to overcome it. I wonder if I ever will.

After the Storm

We lead a humdrum, boring and predictable existence. There are no highs or lows. No exciting adventures or night-time escapades. No earthquakes and no storms. No, I am wrong. We did weather a storm once. Luckily, it passed peacefully. No one was hurt.

We live in a small town, called Sikandrabad. I will not blame you if you have never heard of it. I wouldn't have either, if I did not happen to live here. It is in Bulandshahr district in Uttar Pradesh, not to be confused with the similar sounding, Secunderabad, Hyderabad's twin city. Sikandrabad is not far from Delhi, only 51 km in fact, but it is a different world altogether. It was built by Sikander Lodi of the Lodi dynasty. I have read about him in history textbooks. But of all the Lodi memorials, I prefer Lodi Gardens. The gardens are beautiful, and there is so much history attached to them. We go there whenever we visit Delhi, not because we are lovers of history but because one of my aunts lives on Lodi Road.

Delhi to me is what New York is to others. I am not as grounded as my elder siblings, Smita and Rohit. I live in a world of fantasy. I want to study abroad, join NASA and become an astronaut. After all, if Kalpana Chawla could, why can't I? I have the right to dream. I am only fifteen and for me, the sky is the limit. But Sikandrabad is limiting. It is a town with a population of 3.8 lakh. Compare it to India's population of 1.3 billion, and you get what I mean.

We are a middle-class family. I know that it is fashionable for everyone to claim to be middle class; it gives everyone a badge of respectability, but we really are middle class. Papa is the principal of a degree college, although in my wilder moments I imagine that he is a RAW agent and this job is just his cover. My mother is the vice principal of a convent school, but to me, she is a modern-day Mata Hari.

I need to do this. I need to create an imaginary world for myself, because, as I said before, we live a humdrum existence. Nothing exciting ever happens here.

There are very few chances that I will actually fulfil my dreams. I am not gifted, unlike Smita. I hate to call her 'di' since she is only one year older than me. I wish my parents had considered better family planning. Then I drop that line of reasoning, because if they had adhered to it, I would never even have been born. Smita is everything that I am not. She is fair and petite, barely 5 feet 2 inches, while I am 5 feet 7 inches tall already, and I am still growing. She has a porcelain complexion, while my face is the colour of freshly kneaded dough. She even has dimples; I have acne. She has tawny eyes, just like Mona Lisa's in the poster that hangs on our bedroom wall. I have dark brown eyes, which all other Indians have. I mean, just how unfair can life be? I look just like my father, which is a pity. No, he is not ugly, far from it. But whatever looks good on a man doesn't necessarily look good on a girl.

My elder brother, Rohit, looks like Ma. What luck. Smita

di does not resemble either of them, I suppose she has taken the best of both. I hate it when people ask, 'Are you sisters? We would never have guessed!' I am sure they don't mean it unkindly. Nevertheless, it stings.

Smita excels at everything she does, be it academics, music or painting, and she does it effortlessly. Surprisingly, she envies my height and also my prowess in sports.

'You score a goal in basketball simply by stretching your hand,' she says wistfully. 'I can't even run properly. I am flat-footed.' Maybe we all have our crosses to bear. Having an elder sister is considered a blessing, although I find it difficult to conceive of it that way.

I hold a grouse against Ma because she discriminates between us. I had once tried to raise this issue with her. It had begun innocently enough. 'Kriti,' Ma had said, 'I am dying to have tea, will you make me a cup?' She had just returned from school and seemed drained of all energy. But I too had returned tired from school, I thought truculently—'Make it yourself,' I wanted to say, but I desisted. In our family, one doesn't talk back to one's parents. One obeys. I got up with a flounce, went into the kitchen and made the tea grudgingly.

I thought about it all day and at dinner that night, I could not resist.

'Why don't you tell Rohit da or Smita di to do anything? Why do you always pick on me?'

'I treat all of you equally,' Ma said, her voice strident.

'Oh sure,' I jibed.

Rohit da snorted.

Smita smiled her enigmatic Mona Lisa smile.

'What do you think, Smita?' Ma said, turning to Smita as

though she was not just my elder sister, but the repository of all wisdom.

'I think, Ma,' she said equably, 'Kriti thinks that you favour me.'

'Ha,' said Ma. Our family excels in speaking in monosyllables. Papa remained silent. He had perfected the art of keeping quiet long ago. Now that she had provoked me, I continued with my tirade. 'Smita twists you around her little finger; she gets away with doing nothing. You call me to the kitchen throughout the day. I think I am adopted,' I said petulantly, after a minute.

'Thank God you know now.' Rohit da chuckled.

'Rohit!' Papa glared at him.

'Am I?' I asked Ma, feeling horror-stricken at the thought.

'Of course not,' Ma said promptly. 'If we had to adopt, why would we choose you?' She smiled to take the sting out of the words. Ma has a weird sense of humour. 'Smita is now in Class 10 and has to appear for her board exams next year,' Ma said by way of explanation. She made it clear that while Smita was preparing for her examinations, she would be exempt from doing all chores.

I wondered if there was a law against discrimination. If I found one, I could file a case against Ma. If my bid to become an astronaut at NASA failed, I promised myself, I would become a lawyer and avenge myself.

Having Smita for an elder sister has its advantages. Like the time we wanted to watch the movie *Badla*, which was running in a theatre in Bulandshahr. We didn't think Papa would allow us to go.

But Smita smartly walked up to Papa and said, 'Papa, we want to see *Badla*, which is running in Bulandshahr.'

Papa began to frown, as though she had said Berkeley and not Bulandshahr, and said, 'How can you go? This is your board year, shouldn't you be studying?' But Ma intervened, as she always does on Smita's behalf, and said, 'Let them go, Mohit, Smita needs a break from her studies.'

Papa agreed grudgingly, but only on the condition that Rohit da accompanied us. He even allowed Rohit da to drive us in the car, just because he had turned twenty-one. As I said, Smita can twist anyone around her little finger. Not just my parents but Rohit da as well. He seems like putty in her hands, as do my aunts. Maybe it is not true and I am just jealous.

Papa does not have a brother. Well, not any more. His younger brother, my Raghav Chacha, died many years ago, much before Smita and I were born. Chachi died soon after. Their photograph stands on our mantelpiece, with a sandalwood garland around it. Papa doesn't like to talk about them. Maybe he has never been able to get over their deaths. I wouldn't know about grief. Maybe the dictum 'Time is a great healer' is not really true. We only know what Papa has told us.

Raghav Chacha was travelling, standing on the last step of the local train in Delhi, when he was pushed out of it, accidentally, I am sure. His head hit a pole as he fell on the tracks. He died instantaneously. Maya Chachi died a year later.

'Didn't they have any children, Ma?' I asked.

'No,' said Ma shortly, 'they were married for just a year.'

'Time enough to have a child, don't you think?' asked Smita. Ma smiled a little wistfully.

The monotony of our predictable life was broken when Papa's sisters visited us unexpectedly. They informed us that they were in Greater Noida, which was just 23 km from Sikandrabad and could not miss the opportunity to meet us.

'Have they mistaken Sikandrabad for Srinagar?' I asked grumpily when they rang.

'Kriti.' Ma's voice was stern. I knew that she would not brook any insolence, not when there were guests on the way. I kept quiet. I knew what would happen when they arrived. Papa would retreat further into his shell; Ma would disappear into the kitchen to make delicacies; I would help Ma in peeling vegetables, kneading the flour and washing utensils, even though we have part-time maids to do these chores. Smita would bury her face in her books and pretend that she was studying, while Rohit da would hide in his room on the pretext of studying for his exams.

Radha Bua and Sita Bua arrived half an hour later. Along with them was Rama Bua, Papa's second cousin who I don't think I had ever met.

They slumped on the sofa, which began to sag under their combined weight. Ma offered them nimbu pani. She should have called it a virgin mojito, I thought, just to shock them. Smita entered the drawing room just then.

Rama Bua, the one who had tagged along with my other Buas, took one look at her and said, 'Smita, you are the spitting image of your mother.'

I frowned. Smita did not look like Ma. It was Rohit da who did. I thought somebody would correct her. Instead, a stunned silence descended in the room. Rama Bua seemed surprised and a little embarrassed.

'You haven't told her, have you, Suvarna?' she said at last to Ma. 'I am so sorry. I had no idea.' Ma's face had turned pale. Papa seemed to have turned into stone. Rohit da slumped on a stool. Staring at their reactions I wondered what she meant. Then I saw Rama Bua's eyes fixed on Raghav Chacha and Maya Chachi's photograph and I knew.

I did not dare to look at Smita. For her to have to realize that she was an orphan, that she had lost both her parents in childhood must have come as a huge blow. So many things now fell into place. I understood why Papa never turned down any of her requests and why Ma seldom asked her to help with the housework. I understood why Rohit da seemed to dote upon her. I realized why she seemed to be the darling daughter, and I, the neglected child. My parents were overcompensating. I looked at both my parents in turn. It may not have been difficult for Papa to love Raghav Chacha's daughter like his own. After all, they shared a bond of blood. But for Ma to do so, and so graciously at that? My mother was a remarkable woman. It was a pity that I had not realized it until then.

Ma spoke in a rush. 'Smita, I was going to tell you. I just didn't know if you were ready for it. Maya died when you were just seven months old, of a broken heart, I believe. She died after a brief illness, but I think she had lost her will to live. When you entered our house, a mere infant, we thought our family was finally complete. We had a son, and now a daughter as well. When Kriti came along, a year later, I tried very hard not to discriminate between you and her, believe me.'

Smita said nothing. She sat with her shoulders slumped and her head bowed. No one knew what she was thinking. It must have been a terrible shock to her, I thought. Her world must have collapsed after the revelation. Mine certainly would have.

Smita looked up at last. She was smiling her enigmatic Mona Lisa smile. 'Chill, Ma,' she drawled. 'I am not shocked.

I have known it for a long time.'

'Really?' Ma looked perplexed.

'How?' asked Papa.

'As Rama Bua just mentioned, I resemble my mother. I was dusting the photograph on the mantelpiece one day and I felt that Chachi's face looked very familiar. After returning to my room, I looked at my face closely in the mirror and made a guess. I had her tawny eyes and dimples. Kriti looks like Papa and Rohit da looks like Ma. I always wondered why I did not resemble either of you and finally, I knew the reason. I then realized why you both were so protective. You wanted to give me all the love you thought I deserved. It was a beautiful feeling and I wanted to bask in it for as long as I could, so I didn't bring it up either.'

'Your mother was a very beautiful woman,' Ma said generously.

Smita got up and hugged Ma and said, 'So are you, Ma, so are you—both inside and outside.'

As I said before, we had a storm once, but it passed peacefully. No one was hurt.

The Betrayal

Some faces are ravaged by age, some by experience and yet others by pain. The woman before me seemed ravaged by all three. Her hair was grey and frizzled, wisps escaping from the bun she had loosely tied at the nape of her neck. In a way, the woman reminded me of my mother.

This woman had been wounded deeply, as though someone had plunged a knife into her and turned it, slowly. I knew that she was a widow. She wore a white saree but no bindi or sindoor. There was something about her that told me it was not merely the loss of her husband that she grieved. There were lines of anger etched sharply on her face.

'What happened to her,' I wondered, *'what brought her here to Haridwar?'*

I was sitting on a stone bench outside the dharamshala where I was lodging, when she came and sat beside me. She didn't speak. We sat in silence for a long time. When I turned to look at her, I felt as though her face had been carved in stone, like the faces of the American presidents in the Rushmore mountains. I was taken aback by my own simile.

Then, I noticed a tear trickle down one eye. I did something I didn't think I was capable of.

I gently put my hand on her shoulder and spoke in a calm voice. 'Tell me what is troubling you, Amma, consider me your son.'

She brushed my hand away and said, her eyes blazing, 'Don't call yourself my son.'

I recoiled in horror on hearing the raw anger in her voice. Had I touched a sore spot? I imagined that her pain was related to her son. Maybe she could not imagine anyone taking his place. Was he a soldier who had died on the battlefield? Or a police officer who had laid down his life in the line of duty? She must have been very proud of her son, that is why she could not bear the thought of anyone else trying to take his place.

Trying to disguise my hurt I spoke once again. 'I'm sorry.' But her words still rankled, so I got up and went for a walk. I needed to clear my head and get over the snub. Here I was, a doctor working in a hospital in Chicago, who had come to Haridwar to immerse my father's ashes in the Ganges. I was devastated by his death. My father was my hero; he had also been a doctor who lived by his ideals, spending his entire life serving the poor. The thought of leaving India in search of greener pastures had never crossed his mind. Losing him was like losing a limb.

Everyone in this world has had to face some loss. The old woman before me was no different. How did she abrogate to herself the right to insult me?

I walked through the congested gallies and the paan-splattered roads, sidestepping the mountains of half-eaten chaat, avoiding the half-covered potholes, holding my breath while passing mounds of human excreta, avoiding the shops where sarees and striped cotton shirts were being sold at ₹200 each. I continued walking for an hour and then returned to the dharamshala after dusk.

I was surprised to find the woman still sitting on the same stone bench. Since I had nothing better to do, I went and sat on another bench, a little further away. I was startled by the sound of her sobs. This time, I decided not to intrude. I did not wish to be insulted by her yet again.

From a distance, I saw her holding a photograph. Suddenly, a gust of wind blew it out of her hands. She ran after it, but it continued to float in the air. Suddenly, she stumbled and fell. I hesitated, wondering if I should rush to her side and risk being snubbed yet again, but before I made my decision, I saw her get up and dust her knees. She turned towards me and said something inaudibly. But I knew what she meant.

I did not think twice before picking up the photograph which lay at my feet. It was a photo of a palatial house before which stood the same woman along with a man, probably her husband. The words 'Yashodhara and Shriram' were scribbled at the back of the photograph. I hate to admit it, but I was impressed.

When I returned the photograph to her, she snatched it from my hands and put it into her purse without even thanking me. I had never met a woman as rude as this Yashodhara.

I had planned to return to Delhi the next morning, after the aarti was over. The next morning, when Yashodhara got up for the aarti, she suffered a dizzy spell. She tried to hold on to something to balance herself but failed to do so and fell down on the dhurrie and fainted.

I immediately rushed to her, I do not know why, God knows she had tried her best to keep me away. I lifted her in my arms but she began to stir and asked me to set her down.

'Amma, do not resist,' I said, and forgetting my resolve, once again I said, 'I could well be your son.'

'Not my son, not my son,' she said, punching me on my chest, 'not my son, certainly not my son.'

I blinked back the tears. I did not want to cry, not before this woman who had been snubbing me ever since I had met her. I thought of mother, missing me with the same fierce pride.

Suddenly, she saw the tears in my eyes and caught my arm tightly, her nails digging into it, and muttered, 'I would never want you to be my son.'

'Why?' I asked. It seemed as if she had been waiting for me to ask. Immediately after I set her down, Yashodhara began to narrate her story.

'It took one stroke to change my life completely,' she began. 'My husband's death was that catastrophe. It snatched the mangalsutra from my neck and reduced me into an object of pity,' she said.

'I hadn't realized that India is still so steeped in tradition where widows are considered unlucky.' 'Perhaps,' she added satirically, 'widows in India should be grateful that sati was abolished centuries ago and they are no longer burnt along with their husbands. We should be thankful that our heads are not shaved off and we are not bundled off to the Vidhwa Ashram in Vrindavan.'

'My son, Avni, arrived within two days of Shriram's death. His father's death seemed to have aged him suddenly. Perhaps it was because of the responsibilities that had fallen on to his shoulders.

"Heart attack," he announced, clucking his tongue. "What trigged it so suddenly? Babuji was not suffering from heart disease."

'His diabetes made him susceptible,' I said sadly. 'He went away just like that.'

"Amma," Avni said, "You cannot stay here any longer. Come with me to Chicago."

'I refused to leave my home. I said, "This is the house into which I came as a bride and where I spent forty years of my life. I cannot leave it just like that. Your father may have gone, but he lives on in my memories. I see him everywhere. I see him sitting on the rocking chair where he rocked himself to sleep, while reading the morning newspapers. I see him on the couch where he had placed a small pillow for his back while watching the news on television. I see him on the dining table, his coffee in the steel tumbler, eating idli dipped in gunpowder and gingelly oil, smearing the white tablecloth with chutney stains. I cannot go to Chicago leaving everything. Running a household needs a lot of effort. Your father took care of everything. It is time for me to learn."

"Amma," Avni said, looking at me with an admixture of affection and annoyance, "I know just how well you can cope. You depended on Babuji for everything. How will you manage on your own? Come back to Chicago with me," he had pleaded, but I had refused.

'Six months of living without Shriram taught me how difficult it was to live alone. I lived in a palatial house, but did not know how to contact the plumber when the overhead tank leaked. I had no idea when the car insurance or house insurance was due. I had no idea how to pay the house tax.

'When Avni came to visit again he made the same request. "Your home is with us. Why don't you pack all your clothes and come with me?" I finally decided that Avni was right. He helped me to pack my suitcases. The house was sold, and in a few weeks, we were ready to leave.

'At the airport, Avni put our suitcases in two trolleys and wheeled them inside. The rest of the luggage would come by freight. We walked towards the Air India check-in counter. There was a serpentine queue at the counter.

"It will take at least an hour, if not more, for our turn," my son said to me.

I had absolutely no idea that the queue would be so long.

"Why don't you sit in the waiting area?" he said. "I shall fetch you, just before our turn." He then found me an empty chair and told me to wait while he stood in the queue. I sat on the chair, feeling tired, sleepy and lonely by turns. The airport seemed so alien. This was the first time I had actually been inside an airport. Whenever Avni had come to visit us, we had waited outside the airport to receive him. I feared that I would get lost in the crowd. After waiting for a long time, I realized that I needed to use the bathroom. I looked for Avni. Finally, unable to wait for him any longer, I went to look for a washroom. After returning from the washroom, I realized that my throat was parched. I walked to the spot where the paper cups were piled up near the water filter. I poured water into a cup and drank thirstily from it; I splashed the cold water on my face, wiped it with the corner of my pallu and then turned when I heard a cough. Avni, I thought. It was not Avni, but a pot-bellied, middle-aged man who did not resemble him at all.

'I went back to my chair. Avni had warned me that it would take an hour or more for our turn to come. I needed to be patient. I looked at the queue. It hardly seemed to be moving. At this rate, I thought to myself, we were likely to miss our flight. Or was I looking at the wrong queue?

'After some more time had passed, I began to get nervous. A ground hostess, who was passing by, took pity on me. Perhaps she had seen me sitting all by myself for a long time.

"Where are you going?" she asked me.

"To Chicago," I said.

"She was surprised". "By which flight?" she inquired in a hurry.

"Air India."

"But ... the flight left a few minutes ago," she said.

"Impossible," I retorted, "there must be some mistake."

Suddenly, I had a vision of Avni falling ill and lying somewhere. Avni in the bathroom, having a heart attack or a stroke. Avni, trapped in a lift, unable to reach me. Or worse still, Avni dead. My anxiety began to give way to hysteria.

"Search for him, please," I said frantically to the hostess. The ground hostess went to the Air India counter, checked the passenger list carefully, returned and told me, "Avni has left for Chicago by the Air India flight."

'I refused to accept her explanation. "There must be a mistake," I said. "Maybe someone stole his passport."

The ground hostess shook her head sadly and said, "His passport was checked twice, once at Immigration, and before he boarded the flight." Then, unable to look me in the eye, she said, "He cancelled your ticket before he left."

'She then went to the Air India counter and returned with a trolley containing my suitcases. Avni had pushed my trolley into a corner before the check-in. I could not deny it any longer. My son had abandoned me.

"Can I drop you home?' she asked sympathetically.

"Home?" I began to shiver at the thought. Where was the palatial house into which Shriram had brought me after our marriage? I had given the power of attorney to Avni to act upon my behalf. I had sat with Avni when he had negotiated the sale of the house and signed all the relevant papers.

"I have no home," I said stonily. "My son sold my home, stole my money and has now abandoned me."

"Where can I drop you?" the ground hostess asked me gently.

"I have no home to go to," I repeated.

'The hostess took me to her house and said, "Amma, you may live here as long as you like." Tears sprang to my eyes. There was humanity left in this world, after all—even if my own son didn't have any. I had dinner under the watchful eyes of Sania, my hostess, and even pretended to enjoy the bhindi masala and tur dal she served me. As I lay in the guest bedroom, I began to weep. I wept for Shriram who had left me alone in the world. I wept for myself and the sheltered existence I had led, which did not prepare me for this eventuality. And finally, I wept for the fact that I had given birth to a son who was nothing more than a common thief.'

'Where did I go wrong? I wondered,' the woman said wiping her eyes. 'Did the fault lie in my genes or in the environment that he grew up in? This game of self-blame is what brings parents down. They never forgive themselves for the sins of their offspring. Avni is an adult, well aware of what is right and wrong. He is greedy and a criminal. I would like to blame his wife Chandra for my fate. But she alone is not to blame. And, if he did her bidding, then he is not man enough.'

'I cannot imagine how any son could abandon his mother like this. Even a highway robber would have been more compassionate. What did he expect? That some kind soul would lead me to an old age home, to lead my life among strangers, waiting for a plate of dal, roti and sabzi they would serve me, while I talked to strangers I didn't know, telling them how I was cheated by my son of my home and my inheritance? Or did he think that I would go to one of my relations and narrate the sorry saga of my son's betrayal?'

'The next morning, when Sania must have brought tea to my room, she must have found it empty. I shouldn't have left her house so abruptly, but I hate being beholden to anyone. I went to the station and took a train to Haridwar,' she said, gazing at me. 'Every day, I ask God, why me? But I receive no reply. Perhaps even God has no answers. Now do you realize what I meant when I said you were not my son?'

'What will you do now?' I asked her.

'Do?' Yashodhara grimaced. 'I will take Avni to court and get my money back. I may have no house or money but I have relations and friends in high places. Avni has lived in Chicago for years and does not know that my real wealth is not just the property and money that Shriram left me, but the wealth of goodwill he left behind. I will go to our friends for help. But first, I need to heal myself and come to terms with Avni's betrayal. Then I shall announce to the world what he has done to me. I shall see to it that I destroy him. I shall not rest till I see Avni in jail.'

I looked at the woman before me. Her eyes were implacable and her chin jutted out aggressively. I believed every word of what she said. I began to pity Avni. He had no idea what the future held in store for him.

Eureka Moments

*D*on't we all get a Eureka moment? I had mine when my wife Neena began to babble something about the ice sculpture of Lord Ganesh which featured in the *Times of India* supplement that Sunday.

'Isn't this beautiful, Rajesh?' she repeated. I smiled indulgently at her while I ate my French toast. Breakfast on Sunday was a leisurely affair. I usually had an egg white omelette with multigrain bread but today I woke up and wanted to indulge myself. Neena was having upma with coconut chutney. She loved a South Indian breakfast. We were opposites. She chattered all the time; I am a man of few words. I love Neena dearly, but I always complain that she talks too much, and she is the first to admit it. 'I like the sound of my own voice,' she dimples every time I complain.

'See,' she said, pushing the newspaper in front of me. I saw the picture of the Ganesh idol in the supplement. I looked at it in wonder. It was exquisitely carved. That is when it struck me: an ice sculpture would make an ideal murder weapon. If someone had struck Suchitra with an ice sculpture and later thrown it into the swimming pool, they would have then committed the perfect murder.

'Neena, you are a genius!' I said, ruffling her hair, 'God bless you.'

Neena rolled her eyes and said, 'What have I done now?' I couldn't tell her.

When I went back to my office the next day, I called for Suchitra's file. I knew the case well, but I wanted to refresh my memory.

Six months ago, Suchitra, a well-known painter, was found dead in her farmhouse in Mehrauli. Her body was found in her swimming pool. No murder weapon could be located. It could have been an accidental death—for example, if she had been standing on the edge of the swimming pool, she could have fallen backwards, except for the fact that there were injury marks on her forehead. These were not consistent with her fall. Suchitra knew how to swim, but the blow must have stunned her. She had drowned. Whoever had killed her was about to get away with it, unless I could catch him.

I began to feel the weight my profession had placed upon me. Unlike many of my colleagues, I was unable to leave a case unsolved. I needed to find the killer and bring him to justice. I found the chase thrilling and the denouement satisfying, but more than that, I needed to know and feel relieved that justice had been done.

There were a number of people who had come to Suchitra's house that day; the security guard at the gate had given their names to the police. Among them were Suchitra's maid, Madhu, and her driver, Mohan. Besides them, Adhira, a social worker, had come to request Suchitra for a donation. The last man to visit Suchitra was Madan, an acquaintance of hers.

I had spoken to all four of them.

The maid had come in the morning and Suchitra had opened the door for her. She had made breakfast for Suchitra—a frugal one of one boiled egg and toast, along with a cup of black coffee. Then she had become busy in making lunch. Madhu had opened the door when the driver rang and had given him the car keys, which hung in the drawing room. He had been busy cleaning the car. Suchitra had not told him if she wanted to go out that day, but she was impulsive and would often want to leave on the spur of the moment, so it was his duty to keep the car ready for her. Adhira, who represented an NGO dealing with mental health issues, had come to Suchitra with great hope and had returned empty-handed.

'Suchitra was not of a very charitable disposition, I am afraid,' said Adhira, 'although one must not speak ill of the dead. She brushed me off saying that she did not believe in frittering away her wealth on lost causes.'

Based on what I had heard, I had cast Madan in the role of the main suspect. He was the last to come to the house. Madhu let him into the drawing room, and then proceeded to inform her mistress, who was working in the studio. Madhu then left for the kitchen. The driver was in the garage, so nobody had kept track of his whereabouts. When he was first questioned by the inspector, Madan claimed that his was a casual visit, that he had dropped in as he was passing by, but Suchitra was busy with her painting and had not spared more than a few minutes for him. She had not even offered him a glass of water. She was keen to return to her studio. He had left soon after. Neither he nor the security guard could say definitely how long he had lingered.

Suchitra's studio was at the back of the house. The door of

the studio opened towards the swimming pool. Suchitra often liked to take a swim when she was tired from working. I saw a half-finished painting on an easel. She had painted a tribal woman from the North East, wearing her native dress. It was a good painting; there was something very natural about it. Suchitra had made the woman's eyes come alive, and even her wrinkles seemed real.

I sighed, Suchitra had been a really gifted young woman. It was a pity that such a talent had been cut short so abruptly in its prime.

While searching the house for evidence I had found two letters threatening Suchitra. They were written by someone called Madan. The letters were vague. There was mention of the dire consequences Suchitra would face if she went public with the revelations, or if she went to the police, but I could not make out if it was a love affair she was about to expose or some financial fraud. I knew that Suchitra had made no police complaint; none had been received in the police station. But it seemed clear that if anyone had a motive to kill Suchitra, it was Madan.

After learning about the ice sculptures, I visited Suchitra's house once again. This time, I met her sister, Suvira, who had come down from Mumbai and was busy getting Suchitra's belongings packed. Unlike Suchitra, Suvira looked professorial. She had a thin, pinched face and wore black-rimmed glasses. I learnt that she was teaching in SNDT University in Mumbai. Initially, I found her intimidating until I realized that it was just a pose. She was actually quite timid.

'Ice sculpture?' she said frowning. 'I'm afraid I know very little about Suchitra's artistic activities. But let me ask.'

She called for Mohan and Madhu.

'Madam was just learning to work with ice,' said Madhu. 'She worked with it during winter, when she could order blocks of ice. But now that it is getting warmer, she found it difficult to sculpt. The ice melted too easily. She couldn't make very complicated sculptures, but with practice she was getting better and better every day.'

'Did she make any sculptures the day she was killed?' I asked.

Madhu shook her head, a doubtful look in her eyes.

'I do not really know,' she said.

'But she had ordered ice that day,' interrupted Mohan. 'I fetched it from the van outside the gate.' I began to feel elated. No wonder the security guard had not mentioned the van that brought ice, especially since the van had remained outside the gate.

Even if Suchitra had not been able to make a sculpture that day, she had ice in the studio. Her assailant could have hit her hard with a block of ice. I was sure I had found my murder weapon.

At home, I smiled to myself as I mulled over the facts that I had learnt.

'The name Madan has a villainous ring to it,' I said chuckling, 'and the late Madan Puri is responsible for that. He made an excellent villain onscreen.'

'Madan Puri,' Neena frowned and said, 'Amrish Puri's brother?'

I nodded.

'So, every time you meet a Prem, an Amrish, a Shakti or a Ranjeet do you raise your eyebrows and think, "Villain"?'

I smiled. She was right of course. For all I knew, Madan was as pure as the driven snow.

Madan turned out to be Madan Gopalan, a rather sophisticated gentleman who was an art collector. He owned a small art gallery nearby. The case against him was circumstantial at best. We could find no motive, but the fact that he had visited Suchitra that morning, coupled with the fact that we had found Madan's letters threatening Suchitra, seemed sufficient grounds for his arrest and for the charges against him. Of course, Madan denied all the charges.

I felt a sense of excitement when the case came up in the lower court for hearing. To me it appeared to be an open-and-shut case, but I didn't know that the case was likely to be demolished. Madan's handwriting samples had been sent to a handwriting expert who had confirmed that it was not his handwriting.

His report had been sent to the public prosecutor and the defence counsel just a couple of days before the hearing. The report came as a shock to the prosecution. The public prosecutor sought time to examine the report.

The next weekend, I had my second Eureka moment. Again, Neena had something to do with it.

Neena was sprawled on the sofa, her legs stretched out, her pencil in her mouth. She was doing the *TOI's* Sunday crossword puzzle. The quick clues. She had yet to graduate to the cryptic ones.

'Rajesh,' she said, 'what is a twelve-letter word for someone who is able to write with both hands?'

'Ambidextrous,' I said absently, without looking up from the newspaper I was reading. I wondered why she tried the crossword at all if she didn't even know simple words like that. And then it struck me.

'Neena, you are a genius,' I said. I walked up to her and kissed the top of her head. She looked up at me, seemingly puzzled.

'Have you had another Eureka moment?' she asked.

'I have,' I said, squeezing her hand. 'Thanks to you.'

I knew the public prosecutor rather well. We had worked together on many cases in the past. I told him what I suspected. I told him what I had read about ambidextrous people. Only 1 per cent of the population was ambidextrous. Madan could fall among that 1 per cent. Left-handed people who were forced to use their right hands also became ambidextrous, and their non-dominant hand could perform as well as their dominant one. Madan could have written those letters with his left hand, which in his case was the dominant hand. To the handwriting expert, Madan may have given samples of his right-hand handwriting.

On the day of the next court hearing, when he rose to examine the handwriting expert, the public prosecutor asked, 'Have you considered the possibility that the accused is ambidextrous, and that he wrote these letters using his left hand?'

The handwriting expert frowned. He had not considered the possibility. Only 1 per cent of the population was ambidextrous. He was not to be blamed if the possibility did not cross his mind.

But then he was dogged in his persistence that Madan was not ambidextrous.

The public prosecutor then approached the judge with a request. The defence counsel reluctantly agreed to whatever he had suggested. While walking back towards the accused, the public prosecutor suddenly lobbed a tennis ball, straight at him. Madan caught it instinctively with his left hand.

While this was not conclusive evidence, it did prove that

Madan's dominant hand was the left one.

In the meanwhile, we had picked up other samples of his handwriting from his house. We found that in almost all of them his handwriting matched the writing on the letters that were sent to Suchitra. We also learnt that he had hired a painter who made excellent replicas of the paintings of up-and-coming painters, and he sold them as originals to unsuspecting art lovers. Suchitra had been dismayed to find a copy of her painting in an art lover's house. She knew that the original, one of her best-known works, had not been sold. She loved it so much that she had chosen to keep it for herself. While she did not say anything to the art lover, she had asked him who had sold him the painting. When she had learnt who he was, she had threatened Madan with exposure. He in turn, had threatened her with dire consequences.

Once Madan was sentenced to life imprisonment, I heaved a sigh of relief. Cliched though it may sound, I felt that a huge burden had been lifted from my shoulders.

But I give the credit of solving this case to Neena, who I now consider my muse. And now whenever she chatters, I let her go on.

The Ambush

I sat twirling my spoon in my coffee mug, my face pensive.

'Black coffee, no sugar,' Shivani said and I stopped, apologetic. I had my coffee black, with no sugar, as Shivani had just pointed out. I did not need to stir the coffee so vigorously. I had been lost in my thoughts once again.

'Come on, it's Sunday, let's explore our new house,' she said.

'It isn't big enough to explore,' I muttered, but I was wrong. The SP's house in Tamenlong in Manipur was much larger than the SP's house in Ukhrul, which I had just vacated. No wonder Shivani was curious.

'I don't mean the interiors,' she said, 'I mean the surroundings. I've heard that a stream flows right behind the house. I believe one can fish in the stream.'

'If you know how to fish,' I murmured.

But Shivani grabbed my hand and dragged me out of the house. We walked behind the house through the woods until we came to the stream. Shivani was right. The silver-grey stream was beautiful. It flowed gently through the woods and looked like a pearl-grey ribbon from a distance. I wondered if I could sit on its bank for hours and just watch the water flow. It was a pity I was not carrying a handkerchief but I realized that

Shivani had come well prepared. She took out a large red cloth from her handbag and laid it on the ground.

'Sit,' she instructed. I sat down obediently, put my head on her lap and closed my eyes. But all I could see were the faces of Major Arjun Sherawat and Captain Akshat Khurana. I shut my eyelids tight; I hoped the images would go away. But I was wrong. I could not blot them out of my mind.

We returned to the house an hour later. Soon afterwards, the phone rang. My colleague, Arunoday, was on the line. He told me that he was coming to Tamenlong the next day.

'Looking forward to seeing you,' I said, trying my best to inject some enthusiasm into my voice. But I knew that it sounded dull and listless.

As I sat in my armchair, I remembered the trip I had made with Arjun Sherawat and Akshat Khurana just three weeks ago. It was a trek up the Shirui hill. Arjun and Akshat were going and had asked me if I would like to join them. Shivani had been invited too. But when she heard the word 'trek' she looked suspicious.

'Spare me,' she had finally said. 'That much exercise is not good for me. You know I might disappear.'

'You're sure?' I asked. 'Major Sherawat and Captain Khurana will be good company.'

'Wild horses will not force me to climb a mountain just to see a lily,' she said, shuddering delicately. 'I prefer roses anyway.'

I had laughed.

I drove down to Assam Rifles headquarters on a Sunday to pick up Arjun and Akshat. The two climbed into the jeep with me. We drove to the Shirui Kashong peak, which is located at a height of 2835 metres above sea level. It was an arduous climb.

Shivani had been wise to refuse the invitation. The climb would have fatigued her. But I was glad I had come anyway. The Shirui lily was beautiful. We also saw some rare and exotic birds on the mountaintop.

'It's good we made the journey,' Arjun said. 'I will be leaving Ukhrul in about two weeks and would have never gotten the chance to see it otherwise.'

'Neither would I,' said Akshat. Arjun then pulled out a photograph. 'Before I join my new posting, I will marry Jyotsana,' he said firmly. Jyotsana was his fiancée. She looked very serious in the photograph. Her eyes, which seemed to be too huge for her face, were her most arresting feature. I wondered if she ever smiled.

'She is a doctor,' Arjun said proudly. 'We have known each other since childhood.'

Akshat Khurana also took out a photograph of his wife, Amrita.

'She is expecting our first child,' he said. 'The baby is due in September.'

'Virgo?' I chuckled. 'My zodiac sign is also Virgo.'

'Virgo or Libra, who knows, babies seldom come on the expected due date,' said Akshat.

'God, I miss home,' Arjun said. 'I am a thousand miles away.'

We were in different professions but this one thing we held in common. All of us were far from home. I thanked my stars that I at least had my wife by my side.

'You must come home for dinner before you leave,' I told them. Over the two years that I had been posted in Ukhrul we had grown close and become friends. I had no idea that my transfer orders would come before they left Ukhrul. Arunoday and I had swapped postings. There was nothing really surprising about it. The state government transferred officers routinely. Ukhrul was considered a tough district. It was insurgency-ridden, although it was the army which dealt with the insurgency.

I had already completed two years in Ukhrul. It was time for me to move. Tamenlong, my new place of posting, was considered peaceful. It had just one disadvantage. It was far away from Imphal.

'It is cut off from civilization,' I complained. 'It's an eight-hour drive from Imphal.'

'Good,' Shivani had said, 'it means that no one will disturb us.'

'I believe the SP's house is lovely,' she had added, 'and there is a silver stream.' I wondered where Shivani got all her gossip from. She loved eating fish and rice; no wonder she was excited about the stream. Me, I preferred to buy fish from the market. I looked indulgently at her. I knew that Shivani would not miss the shops, the cinema halls and the restaurants she had grown up with, in Delhi. She loved solitude. It took very little to make her happy.

I began packing the moment I received my posting orders. I had to move first, and I planned to leave the next afternoon. It would take me three hours to reach Imphal. I planned to stay the night in the circuit house and leave the next morning for Tamenlong. The eight-hour drive was a prospect I didn't look forward to.

I was glad that we travelled light in Manipur. We had no furniture. The houses we lived in were furnished. We just needed to pack our clothes and the kitchen utensils.

The next day, while I was packing, Arjun dropped in, along

with Akshat. They had heard the news of my transfer and had come to say goodbye. I was a little perturbed when I saw them. Their arrival was inopportune. I realized that it would delay my departure.

'Bhabhiji, something smells good,' said Arjun. I knew that Shivani would ask them to join us for lunch. Before she could say anything, I cut in and said, 'Shivani, will you send three cups of coffee and some biscuits?'

I knew that she would drop everything to make coffee. Domestic help was hard to find in Ukhrul in 1991 and making coffee did not fit into their skill set. Arjun raised his eyebrows.

'I am leaving soon after lunch,' I said a trifle apologetically. 'We will halt the night in Imphal tonight. I have a long journey ahead of me tomorrow.'

They gulped their coffee quickly and said, 'We will take your leave, clearly you are very busy.' I saw them off at the door itself and didn't walk with them till their car. I was keen to return to my packing. A couple of minutes later I heard the gunshots. I ran out of the house, my revolver in hand, unmindful of my own safety. Both Arjun Sherawat and Akshat Khurana lay on the road, their bodies bullet-ridden. They were both dead. The security guard at the gate had seen nothing; it was over in a flash.

In the event, my departure was delayed by a few days. I could not overcome the sense of guilt I felt after they were killed. If only I had invited them to have lunch with me, maybe the insurgents would have gone away without a word. I wished I could have lived my life differently for those last few minutes. Then, I began to wonder if they were really the targets of the insurgent attack or had they been killed by mistake? Was I the intended victim? Were the insurgents intent on killing me before I left the district?

Jyotsana's serious eyes floated before me. I wondered if she would ever marry anyone. I couldn't forget Amrita who was expecting her first child, who would be born posthumously. The child would never see his father. Guilt smote me very hard. After all, I figured, if the insurgents had wanted to kill them, they could have done so before.

Shivani looked at me. 'Still brooding?' she asked.

I nodded.

'Do you know, Akshat was about to become a father.' I said.

She bent down and whispered in my ear, 'So are you. I am pregnant.'

I looked at her in surprise, pleased and full of wonder. I now realized why she had made excuses not to trek up the Shirui hill. That was the best news I had received. At last, I had found a reason to smile.

My friend, Arunoday, arrived the next day. He sprawled on the sofa immediately upon arrival and announced, 'I am hungry.'

As he had not told us when he would arrive, we had already eaten lunch. 'I have some chicken biryani left over,' Shivani said to him, 'along with cucumber raita and mint chutney. I shall heat it up for you.'

He made a face. 'Rice!' he exclaimed. 'I am trying to lose weight.'

Shivani smiled. 'In that case, I shall get you some tea and Digestive biscuits.'

'No, I shall have the biryani,' Arunoday said hurriedly. While eating his biryani, Arunoday updated me on the investigation into the killings of Major Sherawat and Captain Khurana. A hollow feeling grew in the pit of my stomach. I was afraid that Arunoday would confirm what I had begun to suspect, that it was I who had been the intended victim. Arunoday's next words surprised me.

'There is little progress in the case,' he said, 'but an informant told me that the ambush was first planned two weeks before, near the Shirui hills. But you decided to accompany them on this trip. The insurgents did not want to kill you. You were a very popular SP, you know, and a hard act to follow. Thanks to you, Major Arjun Sherawat and Captain Akshat Khurana lived for two more weeks. But their posting orders had been received and they were to leave soon. This time the insurgents tracked them to your house. They made sure that you were not with them when the officers were attacked. They were shot only after you closed the door.' His next words freed me from blame. 'If they had not been shot outside your house, they would have been shot elsewhere.'

I felt a great sense of relief. I still mourned Arjun's and Akshat's deaths but now I knew that I was not responsible. Shivani came and put her hand on my shoulder and I began to relax. One day, I would visit Arjun's fiancée, Jyotsana, and tell her how much he had loved her. One day, soon, I would visit Akshat's wife, Amrita, and meet their child. Perhaps I would see a glimpse of Akshat in his child. But for now, I would enjoy the peace that surrounded Tamenlong, learn to fish in the silver stream behind our house and look forward to the birth of our first child.

Waverly

The ship was sailing towards the coast. I closed my eyes. I could see Waverly, a beautiful house, made of white marble with its wide stone steps snaking down to the beach. I shook my head. What was I thinking? Waverly was no more. How could I have forgotten? Memory plays strange tricks, resurrecting what stands demolished.

I had watched as a large portion of Waverly was demolished before my very eyes, as a huge tidal wave, not unlike the tsunami, had swept over it. I saw Waverly collapse. It could not withstand the fury of nature.

I wondered why I was making the journey now that everything was over. I thought I had put the past behind me. But the past has a strange way of intruding into the present. I put my hand into my jacket pocket and felt the reassuring rustle of paper. The paper was real. It was not a figment of my imagination.

I closed my eyes and suddenly, the years rolled back. As if the last four years had never happened. I was on a ship once again, a luxury liner. I was travelling from Mumbai to Port Blair on a seven-day cruise. It was a leisure trip—for those who are happy to be at sea. Tishya Mausi was not. She was querulous.

I could not really blame her. The sea made her queasy. She was a bad sailor. She lay in bed the day we boarded the ship, moaning and throwing up by turns. It was my job to clean up after her. After all, how many times could I ring housekeeping for help? I was travelling as her attendant. I cleaned up spittoon after spittoon as she continued to vomit. The rancid smell of her vomit floated into our cabin. No amount of room freshener would eliminate it. I too felt like throwing up. But it was a luxury I could not afford.

'Beta,' she called out. She knew my nickname, but she preferred to call me beta. I preferred that too. 'I want some fresh lime soda.'

'Sure,' I said obediently as I trotted off to order and bring it to her.

Although I was Tishya Mausi's niece, the actual relationship was a distant one. I was just a poor relation travelling in the guise of an attendant.

Obedience is a lesson I had learnt the hard way. When you had a cranky, bedridden mother and a drunk for a father, you learnt to be obedient. It kept you out of trouble. It was best to be meek. 'The meek shall inherit the earth,' the Bible said. I hoped it was true, though I wondered if it applied only to Christians.

In school, my years were all about escape. Halfway through college, I escaped. I became a nursing attendant with little qualification, but with a willingness to learn and an ability to put up with bad tempers. But of course, I could not have left my bedridden mother alone. Someone had to shoulder the responsibilities of the household. I had learnt to do so. Then fortuitously, my mother passed away. I use the word 'fortuitous' deliberately, callous though it may sound. Mother's passing provided me with the perfect opportunity to escape once again. And Mummy's distant cousin, Mrs Trivedi, or Tishya Mausi as I called her, stepped in just then.

She had come for Mother's cremation, simply because she had been in town. I saw her eyes light up when she saw me. It was certainly not because of the strong familial bonds she shared with my mother. It was because she was looking for a nurse or attendant to accompany her to the Andamans. She told me that she suffered from diabetes and hypertension. I could hardly believe my ears. It was perfect.

Tishya Mausi was seventy years old. I was wearing an old saree of hers, converted into a kaftan. She told me that it was pure silk. It smelt of old age. Clothes often do, they smell of mothballs and neem leaves and wrinkled skin. I cut the saree and turned it into a kaftan. I am a good seamstress. Tishya Mausi was not happy. But she knew that if I wore a saree I would trip and fall. She gave in with good grace.

On the second day, Tishya Mausi was feeling better. In her case, I believe, it was a victory of mind over matter. She had to get better, otherwise, for her, the entire trip would be wasted. She got up determinedly, called for me in a quavering voice, and with a walking stick in hand, went to the upper deck. I followed. She parked herself on a table near the staircase and ordered a glass of orange juice. I hoped, for her sake, that the juice would not make her nauseous.

We made a pleasant picture. A lady and her attendant. Tishya Mausi had chosen a conspicuous spot. Anyone who came up to the deck needed to walk past us.

The sun went down after some time, and Tishya Mausi

started to shiver. I went to her room to fetch a shawl. I found it a little puzzling since it was not really cold. But I wouldn't know. I was not seventy. I was just twenty-one. When I was returning, I saw her talking animatedly to someone. She smiled as she saw me coming. Although she was a benign woman, for some reason she reminded me of a tarantula about to snap its victim's neck.

The man with her reminded me of a seventeenth-century knight, the kind whose portrait hung in old castles in the United Kingdom. Of course, I knew little of knights and castles, or of the United Kingdom, except for what I had read in books I had borrowed from the school library. I remembered seeing such a portrait in a novel I had read. The man with Tishya Mausi had an aquiline nose and a cleft chin. I could not see his eyes. Seeing me approach, Tishya Mausi smiled and said, 'Thank you for the shawl, beta.'

The man got up when he saw me approach. He was a gentleman.

'Raj Vishwakarma,' he said with a smile. He had kind eyes. I smiled back.

'Would you like a fresh lime soda or a ginger ale?' he asked me.

'Nothing,' Tishya Mausi dismissively said for me before I could say something. He ignored her.

'A pina colada,' I mumbled. If he was surprised by my choice, he didn't say anything. The drink arrived in a long, frosted glass with a slice of pineapple on it. I had only seen pictures of drinks like these; I had never tasted them before. I took a long sip. The taste exploded on my tongue. Was this what it felt like to be treated like a lady? I liked it.

Who knew, one day I might get used to it. He smiled at me once more. I trembled on feeling the warmth of his smile. He may have been two decades older than me, but he was a very charming man.

The next evening, Tishya Mausi snapped him up at dinner time. It was not difficult for her at all. She had parked herself in the dining room since 7.30 p.m. As soon as he entered the dining room, she waved to him excitedly and said, 'Raj, have dinner with us.' He found it difficult to refuse her invitation without seeming churlish. He sat down, a little wearily I noticed. I wondered why she pursued him so ardently. Her intentions became clear in a minute. She was angling for an invitation.

She drew me into the conversation. 'Have you heard of Waverly?' she asked.

I frowned. The name did seem familiar. Then I realized that I was confusing it with Manderley, the name of the house in Daphne du Maurier's classic, *Rebecca*. I confessed that I hadn't. I couldn't blame her for the smouldering glance she gave me. I had effectively stalled that line of conversation. But Mausi was not one to give up so easily.

'It is the most divine place you could know,' she said, 'white marble, with fountains and pebbled paths.'

'It sounds like the Taj Mahal,' I said.

Raj laughed derisively. She looked at him suspiciously.

He quickly changed the conversation to include me. 'You must have a name. I haven't heard it so far.'

Tishya Mausi flushed on hearing him. It wasn't her fault really. She knew me by the nickname my parents had given me, and I had begged her not to call me by that name in public; she couldn't have introduced us. So, I told him my name.

'Lavanya,' I said with pride. I was grateful to my parents for giving me such an unusual name.

'What a beautiful name,' he said. 'I love it.'

'My mother chose it,' I said shyly.

Tishya Mausi was eager to change the conversation. 'How astute of you to compare Waverly to the Taj Mahal, my dear,' she said to me. 'It was also made for love.'

Raj Vishwakarma began to look sardonic once again. The waiter arrived just in time with lobster soup. This was followed by stuffed mushrooms in white sauce, chicken tikka masala, dal makhani and naan. 'Food for the gods,' I said quietly. I would have liked to fall upon the food like a famished mongrel, but I had to maintain decorum. I nibbled at the naan. Raj ate little, but he noticed my hunger. 'You are a growing child,' he said, looking at me, 'eat up.'

Tishya Mausi began to sulk. She may have been thirty years his senior, but she could not bear to see him pay me so much attention. When I began to eat the tiramisu he had ordered, she said, 'I would like to return to my cabin, beta.' She still would not call me Lavanya; but I was glad that she did not call me by my nickname—Putli. I would have been completely mortified.

'Maybe you can come to the deck and join me after Mrs Trivedi retires,' Raj said to me. Tishya Mausi overheard. I suspected that she would find enough menial tasks for me to do to ensure that I would not be able to return. But I was wrong.

'Go up and enjoy yourself,' she said indulgently as soon as she settled into the cabin.

When I came up to the deck, I did not expect Raj Vishwakarma to be there, but he was. It was a balmy night. He was smoking a pipe. I had never really seen a man smoke a pipe, except in films. I had led a very different kind of life in the chawl in Dharavi. People in the chawl drank country liquor and smoked bidis. No one smoked a pipe.

Raj was a reticent man. A man with secrets. I was an amateur psychologist. It turned out that so was he.

'You are not happy,' he said astutely.

'Who is?' I asked, trying to be blasé.

'How old are you?' he asked suddenly.

'Twenty-one,' I mumbled.

'You look younger,' he said with a chuckle, 'not more than eighteen.' I did not take it as a compliment. I knew that he thought that I was gauche.

We strolled on the deck in silence. He did not try to engage me in conversation. He was a man of few words. Perhaps he chose his words carefully. I remained silent but only because I had nothing to say for myself.

The next night there was a ball on the cruise.

'I have nothing suitable to wear,' I told Raj.

'You have your youth,' he said, 'flaunt it.'

Tishya Mausi had retired to her bed but had told me to go and enjoy myself at the ball. When they announced that a game of Housie was to begin, I looked at Raj in desperation.

'I don't know how to play the game,' I mumbled.

'Let's go for a walk instead,' he said.

'But it's raining,' I protested.

'Have you never walked in the rain before?' he asked quizzically. He picked up an umbrella from the stand and walked out. I felt the rain splash across my face as I ran after him.

'You must prepare for a deluge when you reach Port Blair,' he said lightly. We stood by the railing, and he spoke nostalgically of Port Blair and the Cellular Jail where freedom fighters had been imprisoned. 'You must have heard of Kala Pani,' he said.

I shook my head. I knew so little. I was ashamed of my ignorance. But Raj Vishwakarma just smiled.

'I forget how young you are,' he said. 'I have no idea what they teach in schools these days.' He then narrated tales of valour and the indomitable spirit of the revolutionaries who had spent years in Kala Pani. But he didn't talk of Waverly. Raj Vishwakarma knew how to spin words. He was a master storyteller when the mood got him. Most of the time though, he liked to be alone with his own thoughts.

The night before we reached Port Blair, we were taking another walk when he lifted my chin and said, 'I am much older than you, Lavanya, but I want you by my side for the rest of my life. Will you marry me?' I was stunned.

All I could think was that his proposal offered me an escape from the grinding poverty, which seemed to be my fate, from my drunken father and from the dirty alley in which I had always lived. Why had Raj proposed to me? He could not be in love with me. He had not mentioned love when he had proposed to me. In any case, I did not believe in fairy tales.

Tishya Mausi was ambivalent when I broke the news to her. 'I am happy for you,' she said. 'Raj is a good man, and he has been very lonely ever since his wife Rita died seven years ago. You can't make a better match. But who will look after me?' It did not come as a surprise to me to learn that Raj had been married before. But Rita was dead. And seven years is a long time to get over someone's death, I told myself.

Raj was callous when he heard her complain. 'I am sure you'll find someone else,' he said.

After we docked, I went with Tishya Mausi to her house in Port Blair. It didn't even cross my mind to invite my father to my wedding. Raj and I were married in a temple in Port Blair. It was a quick and quiet ceremony, with just a few of Raj's friends in attendance.

Raj took me to Waverly after we were married.

'This is Mrs Dhaiya, my housekeeper,' he said, introducing me to a woman with a swarthy complexion. Mrs Dhaiya gave me a cursory glance and dismissed me as someone inconsequential. Class always tells, and she knew instinctively that I was lacking.

Raj was a busy man. I had not realized just how busy he was. He was only free from work by dinner. But he was a passionate lover and that made up for his absence during the day.

A week after we arrived, he told me to get ready.

'Where are we going?' I asked, unable to restrain my curiosity.

'To the sound and light show at the Cellular Jail,' he said.

We sat in the first row, and Raj held my hand as the lights dimmed and the commentary began. I was transported into another world altogether, but unfortunately it was not a pleasant one. The stories about Kala Pani were stories of hardships and torture, of the indomitable human spirit, of the love for one's country, of survival against all odds. I heard tales of Veer Savarkar, Batukeshwar Dutt, Yogendra Shukla and Jaydev Kapoor, names I had never heard before. I realized that my own hardships paled in comparison to the hardships these men had suffered. I returned home mulling over all that I had heard. I was sure there were books in Raj's library about these men. I decided that I would spend my time reading about them.

Throughout the next week, Raj kept busy. He warned me

that work kept him preoccupied all the time. He told me that he had started his business by promoting artefacts and handicrafts of the Andamans. It had not been easy, he said, to find markets in India. Surprisingly, the handicrafts were very popular abroad. He had expanded his business and began making furniture with brass inlay work. He had set up factories in different parts of the country.

'You will have to amuse yourself while I am at work,' he said.

The prospect did not dismay me, not as much as he feared that it would. I had many options. I knew that I could spend hours in the library itself. I also loved stitching and embroidery. I could venture into fashion designing. I could also visit Tishya Mausi when I was bored.

The prospect began to enthrall me, although at times when he was away, I wondered if he had forgotten that I even existed.

One Sunday, at breakfast he said, 'Get ready, we are going to Ross Island today.'

I shivered with excitement. I was transported back to the ship where I had met Raj. Then, a small boat took us to Ross Island. I was disappointed when Raj told me that we had arrived. It had taken us just fifteen minutes to reach the island.

'Ross Island was the headquarters for the penal settlement established by the British,' Raj said. 'It was named after the marine surveyor Daniel Ross. Netaji Subhas Chandra Bose stayed on the island for a few days during the Japanese occupation.'

Raj pointed to the ruins of the bazaar, bakery, church, hospital, cemetery, water treatment plant and the Chief Commissioner's residence. We walked for some time, grateful for the fact that we were alone. Suddenly, I saw a herd of deer moving swiftly among the woods. A peacock flew out from somewhere and danced before us. I clapped my hands in delight.

'I have never seen a peacock dance.' I laughed.

'Lavanya, you are such a child,' he said indulgently, but somehow, I was hurt. I knew that he would always treat me as a child, never as an equal. Not the way he had treated Rita. Jealousy is a strange thing. It warps one's judgement. Jealousy began occupying my thoughts. I often thought of Rita, although she was dead. I now began to wonder what she had looked like. I had seen no photographs in the house, except a photograph of Raj and Rita, in which I could only see her profile. I decided to learn more about her.

I visited Tishya Mausi a fortnight later. She was surprised to see me. She had never quite forgiven me for deserting her, although she seemed happy for my sake. And now she had a claim upon Waverly. She could visit it whenever she wanted.

She was having tea when I arrived. There was a plate of cucumber sandwiches before her along with a plate with slices of red velvet cake.

'It is for you,' she said hastily. 'I was not planning to eat it. I know I am diabetic.'

She was lying of course. She had no inkling that I was coming. I took a slice of the cake. It was delicious.

'Tell me about Raj's first wife,' I said to her bravely.

'You want to know about Rita?' she asked, surprised.

'Describe her to me,' I said.

She remained silent for a long time. I was afraid that she had forgotten what I had asked. Suddenly she spoke. 'Flamboyant,' she said.

I was startled. Surely, she was not calling me flamboyant? I considered myself meek and submissive. Then I understood.

She was describing Rita.

'She was a beauty,' she added, 'a real stunner.' My heart sank on hearing her. 'Raj always had an eye for beautiful women,' she added.

'Clearly not always.' I grimaced.

'What do you mean?'

'Well, he married me, didn't he?'

'Don't underestimate yourself,' she said sharply. 'You are as beautiful as Rita, but in a subdued, understated way. If she was a red rose, you are a white one. As for me, I love white roses.'

I was speechless. I had never considered myself beautiful.

That same evening, I asked Mrs Dhaiya for a photo of Rita.

'Why do you want it?' she asked, her eyebrows raised. There was a hint of insolence in her voice.

'Just get me the photo,' I insisted authoritatively. Tishya Mausi's words had bolstered my confidence. She walked upstairs to her room and brought me a photograph of Rita. I gaped. The woman in the photograph was stunning. That was the only word I had. Her eyes were mesmerizing. They seemed to follow me as I moved from one end of the room to the other. She was a flamboyant beauty. I now understood why Raj had fallen in love with her. But I couldn't understand why Raj had married me. Was he moved by compassion? Or pity? Whatever it was, after seeing Rita's photograph, I knew that it couldn't be a shred of love.

'How did she die?' I asked Tishya Mausi the next time I visited her. 'She died during the tsunami in 2004. Don't you remember reading about the tsunami? She was out on the beach the morning the tsunami hit the island.

That evening, I mustered courage and asked Raj about Rita.

I was afraid that he would be angry, but he was not.

'Rita was temperamental and moody, highly strung and mercurial. I loved her all right, but I found it very draining to live with her. The day she died, Mrs Dhaiya saw her leave for the beach. I was busy completing my painting in the garden. I find painting very relaxing. That is how I unwind. Then the tsunami struck. Luckily, we were otherwise safe since Waverly is built at a height.

'Her body was never recovered. She was declared missing, not dead. It was awful, not knowing. I had to wait for seven years before I could think of getting married again.'

I didn't ask Raj if he loved me. I did not want to know. It was enough that he had married me.

'Mrs Dhaiya doesn't like me,' I said casually.

'That's just her way,' he said. 'She has become morose and depressed since Samay died.'

He did not say who Samay was. 'How did he die?' I asked. 'He jumped off a cliff. She was beside herself with grief.' Raj's response was laconic. Definitely a son, I thought. No husband deserved this kind of grief. I was becoming a cynic. Was there a mystery behind Samay's death? Talking to Raj had assuaged my curiosity about Rita and Raj. Now I was sure that Raj was not pining for her. I thought that Raj had put the past behind him.

And then, it happened again. The supercyclone, like the tsunami earlier, hit Port Blair once again. Portions of Waverly crumbled and fell, and when they did, they smashed the basement as well. The basement revealed Waverly's dark secret. A skeleton. The forensic expert to whom the body was sent confirmed that it was Rita's. The body which the tsunami had supposedly swept away had actually been hidden in the basement all these years. Mrs Dhaiya said that Rita had gone to the beach that morning. When had she returned, and who had killed and buried her? The police believed that it was Raj. They took him into judicial custody.

'I didn't do it,' he protested.

To me he said, 'I don't know who did it, but trust me, Lavanya, I did not kill Rita.'

But, in my gut I knew that it was Raj who had killed his first wife. Who else could have done it? Mrs Dhaiya had been beside herself with grief when she thought that Rita had been swept away in the tsunami. There could be nobody but Raj, and although I loved him and was married to him, I could not live with a murderer.

'Please don't leave,' he said when I told him that I had packed my bags. I refused to look him in the eye. I returned to Mumbai and to my dreary life as an attendant. Alongside it, I took night classes and graduated from university.

A few months after I had arrived, Tishya Mausi wrote to inform me that Raj had been released from prison soon after I had left. He had an alibi for the morning of the tsunami.

'Justice can be bought,' I said to myself, 'and Raj is a rich man.'

Three years later, my humdrum existence was rocked once again. This time I received an envelope, which had been sent to me at Tishya Mausi's address, which she had forwarded to me. It was written by Mrs Dhaiya.

'Mrs Raj Vishwakarma,' it read, 'by now, you must know that Raj did not kill Rita. And you may have wondered who did. Well, I killed her. Raj Sir is truly a gentleman. He is incapable of killing anyone. I know that he loved Rita. I thought she loved him too, until I saw her with my son, Samay. Maybe Rita just needed her husband's time and attention, which he was unable to give her. He was too busy taking his business forward. It takes very little for people to stray. Feeling neglected is as good a reason as any.

'Samay was besotted with Rita and overwhelmed when she began paying him attention. They had an affair, when Raj was travelling abroad, and although for Rita it may have merely added some excitement in her rather dull life, Samay read much more into it. He deluded himself into believing that Rita would leave Raj and Waverly to live with him in our little cottage. My son mistook lust for love. When he asked Rita to leave Raj and marry him, she laughed at him.

'She said that he had been influenced by *Lady Chatterley's Lover* and had thought that she, the Lady of the Manor, would leave Waverly to live in a cottage, to be the wife of a farmhand. Samay had thought that she loved him too and Rita had told him that she only loved Waverly.

'Samay could not take the rejection. He jumped off a cliff. His body was found on the beach. No one else knew why he died. No one knew about him and Rita, not even Raj. He was too engrossed in his business and his travels. But I knew about them. I confronted her. But she laughed at me. She called me a hag. She laughed and asked me to jump off the same cliff.

'She felt not an iota of grief about the death of my son. When I heard her speak so dismissively about Samay I snapped. I put my hands around her throat and squeezed. Too hard and well, she died. I hadn't realized just how easy it was to kill someone. I dug up the basement. It took me half the night, but I did it. I put her body underneath and poured wet cement over the floor. I knew that nobody ever came to the basement except me, so no one would ever find out the truth. I was aided and abetted by the tsunami. Nobody saw her on the beach the next day except for me, but nobody questioned me. Raj didn't suspect anything because he had returned late from work and did not want to disturb Rita. In any case, they had separate bedrooms. He was a late riser and believed me when I said that she had gone off to the beach. It didn't surprise him. She did it quite often.

'I never thought that Raj would be arrested for Rita's murder. I felt guilty when he was arrested but I was sure that he would be released immediately as the police had no evidence against him. When he was not, I told the police that I had been busy gardening while Raj was busy painting a canvas, and he had been so absorbed in his work that he had not seen me. He had been nowhere near the beach nor the basement. Of course, no one but me knew that Rita had died the day before. The police did wonder why I had not come forward earlier, but I said that I was afraid that I would be considered a suspect. It was a plausible excuse, and they knew that there is nothing the poor fear more than the police. Raj was released, but people wondered and still do, as they are bound to. No one knows how Rita died and who killed her. There will be no closure for her death until the truth is revealed. I will confess to the police that I did it. I have been diagnosed with cancer and have only a few months to live. I do not want to die without clearing Raj's name. Raj is a good man. Go back to him.'

Mrs Dhaiya's confession came both as a shock and as a relief to me. I had misjudged Raj. I decided to return to Raj immediately.

As I boarded the ship, I wondered where I would find him. There was no Waverly any more. When I reached Tishya Mausi's house, I learnt that Raj had rebuilt the portions of Waverly that had been demolished. I left for the new Waverly immediately and found Raj on the lawn, painting a canvas. He was squinting in the dark. I went and stood behind him. He didn't turn. He was absorbed in his work.

At last, he looked at me.

'You came?' he said. There was wonder in his voice, but no welcome in his eyes. 'Why did you?' he asked. I fumbled. Once again, I was the girl with zero confidence, stuttering and stammering before him.

'This is Mrs Dhaiya's letter,' I said at last, handing it over to him.

He read it as I waited, and then gave a hollow laugh. 'So her words exonerated me.'

The uneasy silence between us began to grow. 'Go back to where you came from,' he said. His voice was harsh. I stole a glance at his profile. It was dark and saturnine. I remembered it as kind.

'*Is that what prison does to you?*' I wondered. Could a few months in prison have done this to him? I blinked hard to stop the tears from falling, but they flowed.

'Spare me the tears,' he said. His tone was still harsh.

He did not ask me to sit. Nevertheless, I sat on the stone bench beside him. He did not say anything. I understood that I had intruded into his life. I was unwelcome. Tears began to fall from my eyes once again. But he was not moved by my tears.

'With love comes trust,' he said. 'If you loved me, you would have trusted me. But you didn't. You returned to Waverly only because you now know that I am not a murderer.'

I was silent. One does not challenge the truth.

'Go back,' he said. 'Three years is a long time. Long enough to rebuild Waverly. Long enough to learn to live alone. Go back.'

How will I? I wanted to ask, but I was sure that Raj was not interested in my questions. There was a lot of hurt in his eyes. A great deal of mistrust. A lot of grief.

I turned away and returned with leaden steps to Tishya Mausi's house. But I was not about to give up. I knew that I would return. Like Rita before me, I could not ignore the pull of Waverly. I loved Waverly and Raj, in that order. I lifted my chin. Like Scarlett O'Hara in *Gone with the Wind*, I too believed that 'tomorrow is another day'.

The Façade

Malini stepped out of the doors of Manila International Airport at 8 a.m., saw the crowd and groaned. She wished she had informed Arijit about her arrival instead of deciding to surprise him. It would have ensured a faster exit. *'What is done is done,'* she thought. She hoped Arijit would be happy to see her, but somehow she doubted it. Whoever had coined the adage 'Absence makes the heart grow fonder' had probably not endured a long-distance marriage.

'Absence does not make the heart grow fonder, it makes the heart wander,' she thought and giggled.

'See you soon,' her colleague Madhav's voice intruded these thoughts. He looked tired. The flight from Delhi to Manila, with a stopover in Singapore, had been exhausting, and they had spent the entire time chatting instead of resting.

'See you tomorrow at 10 a.m.,' she responded, then went to book a taxi. The invite for the week-long training programme in Manila, which she had come to attend, had come as a surprise to her. Trainings were seldom scheduled in the Philippines but she was glad for the opportunity to visit her husband, Arijit.

As she sat inside the taxi, she saw the long line of vehicles before her. Traffic moved slowly. She closed her eyes and immediately fell asleep. She was seldom able to sleep on a plane. Twenty minutes later, when she opened her eyes, she found that she was still at the airport. They had merely moved from Terminal 4 to Terminal 1.

'At this rate, I will take two hours to reach Arijit's house,' she thought.

When she finally arrived there she found his maid, Joyce, cleaning the driveway.

'I'll give her this,' thought Malini, *'she may be a hopeless cook, but she can certainly clean.'*

Joyce's eyes widened with surprise and consternation upon seeing her at the gate. Malini wondered why. She paid the taxi, left her suitcase at the doorstep and went inside the house. Joyce came in hurriedly after her, suitcase in hand.

'Come, Madam,' she said, ushering Malini into the drawing room. It was as immaculate as she remembered it. Clearly, Arijit did not spend much time in it. Suddenly, she heard the sound of laughter from the lawn.

She strode outside.

'Surprise!' she said gaily and then stopped in her tracks. Arijit was sitting in an armchair, draped on his lap was a stunningly beautiful woman. She was actually sitting on the armrest, but somehow the effect was the same. The fact that she was clad in a swimsuit did not help.

'Malini ... what are you doing here?' Arijit stuttered.

'Not the words of welcome for a wife who has flown all the way from India,' said Malini sardonically.

Arijit flinched and the woman hurriedly got up from the armrest. Malini then noticed Sanjeev dozing in the shade.

'The ever-faithful Sanjeev,' she said sarcastically. Sanjeev woke up with a start. Perhaps he had merely been pretending to be asleep, in order to avoid this unpleasantness.

'Roma came here for a swim,' explained Arijit.

'Does her house not have a swimming pool?' asked Malini. 'I'm surprised, I thought every house in Manila did.'

'I must leave, Arijit,' said Roma hurriedly. 'I am getting late for lunch.'

Her departure broke up the party. Sanjeev sauntered upstairs into the guest room, while Malini and Arijit headed towards the bedroom.

'Why does he rent a house when he lives here permanently?' asked Malini.

'Really, Malini.' Arijit laughed. 'He comes only during the weekends.'

'When does Roma come?' she asked angrily. 'Every day? And is she the only one?'

Arijit understood. She was referring to the occasions when she had seen Arijit in the company of the women, although Arijit had always claimed they were business colleagues. Arijit had the grace to blush. Malini flopped on to the bed, and within minutes she was fast asleep. She got up with a start an hour later, when Arijit woke her up.

'Let us go out for lunch,' he said. 'A new restaurant—Banana Leaf—has opened at the mall. They make delicious mushroom in white wine and breads with garlic and green chillies.' Arijit was extending an olive branch; Malini was too hungry to refuse.

'Sounds good,' Sanjeev said when Arijit told him what he had planned for all of them.

'At least I will not have to suffer Joyce's cooking,' said Malini.

Arijit recalled the last time Malini had visited Manila. That was three years ago. He had heard Malini shouting at Joyce and had seen Joyce walk out of the kitchen in tears. He had tried to placate Joyce. 'You know my wife's temper,' he had said conspiratorially, 'but don't worry, Joyce, she will leave in a week.' Joyce had giggled. Malini had overheard them. She had cut short her visit and returned to India the next day.

'How could you support Joyce instead of me?' she had asked when Arijit had called later. She had not returned to Manila until now.

That afternoon, along with Sanjeev, Arijit and Malini walked down to K&R Negosyo Mall, close to Corinthian Gardens, where they lived. As Malini dug into the mushrooms at Banana Leaf, she sighed. This would have been her idea of bliss, but for Sanjeev's presence. She couldn't blame Arijit for bringing Sanjeev along since he was a house guest. She looked at Arijit's well-sculpted face and then at Sanjeev's flabby one. Why did she dislike Sanjeev so much? Was it because of the lines of dissipation on his face? Or was her gut telling her that Sanjeev was not good for Arijit? Maybe she blamed Sanjeev for encouraging Arijit to join the Asian Development Bank, after he himself had joined. That was eight years ago.

After a leisurely lunch, they returned to Corinthian Gardens.

'We must invite my colleague Madhav for a meal while I am here,' she said. 'The only problem is that Joyce can't cook.'

'Why not call him over for lunch at the ADB?' suggested Arijit.

'I'll see,' she said. 'Maybe we can figure something out.'

That night as Arijit turned towards her, she yawned.

'God, I am tired,' she said.

'Come on, Malini,' he said with a laugh, 'you cannot make

excuses tonight. Remember that I am a lawyer and can take you to court for the restitution of conjugal rights.' She smiled up at him.

'Why do you think I opted to come to Manila for training?' she murmured.

The five days of training passed quickly. Malini had not anticipated that the training would be so rigorous. Malini arrived with Madhav for the promised lunch at the ADB on the last day, having decided to miss the field trip.

'This is just like the World Bank,' Madhav said as he picked up a tray and headed for the section on Indian cuisine.

'Have you been to the World Bank?' Arijit asked.

'I was posted there for five years. Did Malini not tell you?' Madhav inquired. Arijit was silent. It was obvious that the visit to the ADB had left Madhav unimpressed.

'I wish you would stay longer,' said Arijit, a day before Malini was to depart. 'You come to Manila so rarely.'

'If you hadn't left India to join the ADB,' she said, 'we wouldn't have suffered a geographical separation.'

'Distances can be bridged, Malini,' said Arijit, sombrely, 'provided one makes the effort.'

That evening, Arijit left home for some last-minute shopping. Malini sighed. She knew that he would drive to the mall and buy her a bottle of Chanel No. 5 and a Louis Vuitton bag. It would be his peace offering. Arijit had been doing that for years.

She decided to use this time wisely.

She strode confidently towards Sanjeev's room and knocked.

'Come in,' Sanjeev muttered. He was lying in bed in his pyjamas. Perhaps he had been expecting Joyce and was startled to see Malini. She decided not to waste time on social niceties.

'Is Arijit having an affair with Roma?' she asked. She was nothing if not direct.

Sanjeev was shocked. 'What kind of a question is that?' he stammered.

'A straightforward one,' Malini said sharply.

'Frankly, I wouldn't know,' he said. 'I am not his keeper, you know.'

'Really,' she said, her eyebrows raised, 'you both have behaved like Siamese twins, ever since I have known Arijit. I dare say that if you had your way, you would have accompanied us on our honeymoon!'

'Don't be silly, Malini,' Sanjeev said. 'Your remark isn't funny. If Arijit is sleeping with Roma, you have no one but yourself to blame.'

She glared at him, but he carried on, undeterred.

'You left Arijit in Manila for seven years, and you know what kind of a place Manila is …'

'What kind?' She grew quiet. Sanjeev wondered which was more frightening, her loud slightly hysterical voice, or her quiet one. The latter, he thought. 'In the meanwhile,' he continued, 'you have let yourself go.'

His eyes raked her mercilessly, but there was nothing lascivious about his gaze. Malini knew that he was referring obliquely to the twenty pounds she had accumulated over the last fifteen years of her marriage. *'Nothing that six months in a gym cannot fix,'* she thought to herself.

'Why don't you chuck up your job in India and join him in Manila?' he asked.

'It isn't just a job, Sanjeev,' she said, 'it is my career. I cannot throw it away and come to Manila to keep an eye on him, simply because his libido works overtime.'

Sanjeev realized that her temper was rising, and he quailed. He had seen Malini in a rage before. Once she had swept Arijit's priceless crystals off the mantelpiece, at another time, she had slashed his favourite canvas with a pen.

Suddenly, Malini's mood changed. She looked almost pensive.

'I am a civil servant,' she said proudly. 'I cannot give everything up because Arijit gets randy whenever he sees a beautiful girl.'

Sanjeev knew that Malini disliked him; she had never forgiven him for the fact that Arijit had left his successful law practice in India and followed him into the ADB, forcing an unanticipated geographical separation between them.

The meal that night was a silent one. Malini thought about the growing distance between Arijit and herself. *'Seven years is enough time to drift apart,'* she thought. Surprisingly, she had no regrets. Her life was in India and his was in the Philippines. Perhaps they would continue this way until they retired. Or they would drift further apart.

The next day, Arijit offered to drop her to the airport, but she told him Madhav would pick her up on his way there.

'You are sure that you do not want me to come to the airport?' Arijit asked again as Malini got into the taxi. *'Perhaps he really misses me,'* she thought as she waved goodbye.

That night, after dinner, Joyce retired to the servant room. Arijit and Sanjeev walked upstairs casually. Sanjeev stood beside Arijit's bed, his eyes on Arijit. *'There was something so irresistible about him,'* thought Sanjeev. Was it his cleft chin or the dimples that flashed whenever he smiled? Maybe it was his blue-grey eyes, unusual in an Indian. No woman could resist Arijit, nor could any man. Sanjeev sighed. He was lucky to have him. He poured olive oil on his hands and with slow sensuous movements, began to massage Arijit's back.

'Don't,' Arijit said, 'you know I cannot resist this.'

'I know,' Sanjeev said, smiling a little as he continued to massage him. Arijit began to moan gently.

'You needn't have said what you did to Malini,' Arijit said, turning on his back suddenly. 'You know there is nothing between Roma and me.'

'That was the only way I could deflect her attention from *us*,' Sanjeev argued defensively, 'especially after the jibe she made about our being like Siamese twins. I was so afraid that she would begin to suspect and figure out that you prefer men.'

'Or at least one particular man,' said Arijit, as he grabbed Sanjeev playfully and pulled him closer.

Suddenly, the knob turned.

'Sanjeev, did you not lock the bedroom door?' Arijit asked, gaping at the woman standing there. Sanjeev was suddenly conscious of his protruding belly and the trousers he had casually tossed on the floor.

Malini stood there in surprise. Then, she recoiled in horror. She rushed to the bathroom and puked in the washbasin. She could hear Sanjeev's swift indrawn breath and the word 'Shit'.

For a few minutes, Arijit and Sanjeev sat immobile, alert to the sound of water running in the basin. Then, she returned.

'Years of subterfuge and lying. Creating the image of a Don Juan. That was a part of the smokescreen, a façade behind which you have been hoodwinking me all these years?' Malini shrieked.

Arijit was the first to get over the shock of Malini's

unannounced return into the house. She had probably come in with the extra pair of keys he suspected she had purloined from his desk. He watched her turn to Sanjeev.

'I took your advice, Sanjeev, and I decided to chuck my career. I wanted to save my marriage at any cost. I did not board my flight and returned from the airport. While returning, I was afraid I would find Arijit with Roma. But what do I find?' she asked, 'that my husband is gay?'

'Malini …' he began. And she stopped crying suddenly.

'I could compete with a woman,' she said. 'How can I compete with a man?'

Arijit had the grace to blush.

'My marriage was a façade, wasn't it? Gay relationships were banned in India fifteen years ago?' she asked, 'and all the subsequent women that you flaunted, were merely red herrings, to draw my attention away from your gay lover?'

Arijit did not respond.

'Imagine what will happen when Papa finds out,' she sobbed.

Arijit blanched ocn hearing her. He did not know whether she was referring to her father or her father-in-law.

'Stop it, Malini,' he said, dreading the prospect of his affair with Sanjeev becoming public. He knew that he would not be able to live down the scandal. It would affect his job and his life.

'Now that you know the truth, tell me, what you want?' he asked quietly.

'I want out,' she said directly.

Relief flooded his face. He was ready to grant her a divorce. Their fifteen-year-old marriage had already proved to the world that he was heterosexual.

'Being your wife, I will get half your assets,' she added.

He nodded slowly. He realized that he had no choice but to accept her terms, whatever they were.

'And, I will not spend another night under the same roof as you,' she said.

Before he could heave another sigh of relief she said, 'I will stay in this house tonight. You should book a hotel for yourselves.'

Arijit and Sanjeev did not dare to argue with her.

Malini laughed softly after they left.

'Fools,' she said out loud in the empty house. 'Did Sanjeev really think that he had convinced me that Arijit and Roma were having an affair?'

For years she had suspected that Sanjeev and Arijit were lovers and now she had proof. She would get a quick divorce and half of Arijit's wealth. After a few months at the gym, she would be as slim as she had been at the time of her marriage. And Madhav, her colleague, with whom she was in love, and who, she guessed, reciprocated her feelings, would soon be free to propose to her.

'Dear Madhav,' she thought to herself. Down to earth, unassuming and brilliant, who admired her from afar because she was married. And if he didn't, Malini smiled to herself, she would make the offer herself.

She was a liberated woman after all.

The Gold Chain

There was something ominous about the morning.

It is easy for me to say that on hindsight, but I confess I got up that morning with a sense of foreboding. The reason for my trepidation was that after my four-day trip to Wayanad, I suspected that I had a serious heart problem. I was suddenly conscious of my own vulnerability. I was nearing fifty, the age every woman dreaded.

In Wayanad, I had my first inkling that something was wrong with me.

As I climbed up the three storeys to the observation tower in the Wayanad Wildlife Sanctuary, where I had hoped to spot wild elephants, I had begun to pant. The next day, when I had walked down the rough-cut steps towards the man-made lake, I had again gasped for breath. Naturally, I was worried. People were known to die during their first heart attack and women were as vulnerable as men once they reached menopause.

I could imagine myself collapsing due to an undiagnosed heart problem.

When I woke the next morning, I decided to go to Lodi Gardens for a walk. If I was able to complete it without a problem, I would know that I was merely out of shape. If not,

I would have to find a cardiologist.

I smiled and waved when Gautam walked in just as I was about to step out. His body had been glistening. He had probably gone to the India Habitat Centre for an early morning swim.

'But it didn't open so early,' I thought, as I began walking towards Lodi Gardens.

Suddenly, I felt a strong force on my neck. The chain I wore rubbed against my neck, the edges digging into my flesh as I found myself dragged back uncomfortably. Then, the chain was pulled off my neck. Instinctively, I began screaming,

'Chor chor!' I said, gasping, *'Pakdo, pakdo!'*

There were people walking ahead of me, as well as behind me. But no one chased after the chain snatcher. As he boarded a motorcycle, I decided I should take his photograph. I then discovered that the iPhone I wore in the pouch around my neck had been stolen as well.

'Foolish of him,' I thought. I had noted the IMEI number and whenever the chain snatcher started the phone, the police would be able to find out. I rubbed my neck. The abrasion hurt. I was shocked to find that it was bleeding.

With leaden steps, I returned home. I was no psychic. Yet I had known that there was something ominous about that morning.

While returning, I met Rasika, a police officer with whom I had a nodding acquaintance.

'Rasika,' I said urgently on seeing her, 'my gold chain has been snatched. Please help me lodge an FIR.'

Rasika was shocked to see the blood dripping from the abrasion.

'You need medical attention first, Garima,' she said. I ignored her advice.

'Just help me lodge the FIR,' I repeated.

Rasika walked with me to my house. Gautam came to the door on hearing my voice, and felt faint on seeing blood.

'How? When? Where?' he said, his voice faint.

'This is no time for explanations,' I said testily. 'Don't waste time, just call the doctor.'

Gautam looked chastened while Rasika hastily averted her eyes. Gautam did not deserve to be put down like this. He was my husband and deserved to be treated with respect, but today, I had an excuse.

Rasika helped me lodge an FIR immediately.

'There are gangs of chain snatchers in the city,' said the police officer. 'It is difficult to catch them, but we will try.'

'This is a VIP area, there must be CCTV cameras everywhere,' I said.

'There are no CCTV cameras on this route,' he admitted.

'Even if there are, they are not likely to be working,' quipped Gautam. Both the police officer and I glared at him.

'I have the IMEI number of the iPhone with me,' I said.

'How fortunate,' the officer said. 'It will help.'

'What is an IMEI number?' Gautam asked.

'It's the number through which we can trace the phone once it is switched on,' I explained wearily.

'Won't the thief just throw the SIM card away?'

'That won't matter,' said the officer. 'The IMEI number will help us track the phone. 'But I am less optimistic about recovering your gold chain,' he admitted, turning to me. 'Chain snatchers melt the gold after they have snatched the chain; therefore, the chain is never recovered.'

'That's very heartening to know,' I said sarcastically. He

looked put out by my remark.

'You are lucky to be alive, Ma'am,' he bristled. 'You must remember the case of the woman who had her throat slit during a chain snatching, simply because the chain snatcher was unable to pull the chain from her neck.'

I shuddered. I didn't recall reading anything about such a case.

That night, I lay in bed, unable to move my neck to either side. I have no idea when I fell asleep. When I woke up, I saw Gautam lying next to me, his arm by his side, careful not to touch my neck. I smiled despite my pain.

There was something very young and innocent about him.

I ruffled his hair, careful not to wake him up. His windswept hair, his charcoal-black eyes, long eyelashes and his cleft chin made him a painter's delight. It was a pity he had never posed for a self-portrait.

I knew that he deserved much more success and recognition. It must be galling to be known as Mr Garima Sehgal, my husband, but he had never said anything. It must have been painful to see that while visitors murmured appreciatively about his paintings, that seldom translated into sales. It must be frustrating to watch me snub him publicly. I wish I didn't. I would have to learn to control myself.

I only wished Gautam would stand up for himself, at least occasionally. I closed my eyes. It hurt to think about Ravish. I remembered him as an air force pilot in his uniform, standing on my doorstep. 'Don't worry, Garima,' Ravish had said while leaving, 'I will return safely.' I knew that he would. But he didn't. His plane was shot down. I tried not to think about it. I hoped that he had died quickly. I couldn't bear to think of him dying painfully. I decided not to marry. And I had kept the promise I had made to myself until I was thirty-nine.

Now, I was the owner of an art gallery, which belonged to my father before me. But paintings were not my first love; books were. I was the chief editor of a major publication house.

I first met Gautam at the workplace. He was the artist I was promoting. I saw potential in him. I loved his art works. He was not like Ravish at all, but he had an air of confidence about him. He knew that he had talent. He was waiting to be discovered. After we met, he began to chip away at my resistance. He assured me that age was just a number. It didn't matter that I was thirty-nine and older than him by more than ten years. It didn't matter that my biological clock was running out. He said that he wanted me; he was willing to live without children.

'It will not work. It will not work,' I had repeated to myself for months. It took Gautam two years to persuade me that I was wrong.

We were married eight years ago.

However, Gautam's potential as a painter remained untapped. It upset me to see that. It irked me even more that he did nothing about it. Perhaps artists are like that—moody, unworldly and unambitious. In contrast, I was ambitious, a career woman.

'I have become a house husband,' Gautam would sometimes say. Inwardly, I flinched every time he said that no woman likes it when a man is dependent on her for all his worldly needs. Over the years, my irritation had begun to show, although Gautam, to his credit, seldom retaliated.

The next day, I woke up with a headache. My neck hurt. And I began to look at the world suspiciously.

'I do not believe this was a random chain snatching,' I told

Gautam. 'I think I was targeted.'

'What makes you say so?' he asked in surprise.

'I had not gone there for a walk for four days prior to that, but he was waiting for me, on the fifth. How did he know that I would go for a walk today?' I asked.

'It must be a random chain snatching,' he said. 'It was a heavy chain. The chain snatcher must have spotted it from a distance.'

I was surprised to hear Gautam disagree with me. He seldom did. He was becoming increasingly assertive. In a way, I was glad.

I brought it up again a while later.

'I suspect one of the servants was behind the chain snatching,' I said. 'Perhaps it was our maid, Vasudha.'

'Why would Vasudha ...' he asked.

'Well, I rave and rant at her because she is a lousy cook. I even refused her demand for a raise. Maybe this is her way of taking revenge.'

'You rave and rant at me as well,' Gautam said laughing, 'but do I avenge myself?'

I flushed. He was right, of course. I had a short fuse. 'But could it not be Punita, our cleaning woman? Her daughter is getting married and I am sure she needs the money.'

'It could be the gardener,' said Gautam.

'Or the gardener,' I said, with a noticeable lack of enthusiasm. I liked the gardener.

The chain snatching incident brought a change in our relationship. I became less aggressive while Gautam gained more confidence.

'Garima,' he reassured me repeatedly, 'don't worry. This incident will not be repeated.'

'I wish that were true,' I said, ever the cynic.

Six months later, while Gautam had gone to the India Habitat Centre for a swim, I found his Godrej almirah open. That was unusual. He always kept it locked. I got up for a glance out of sheer curiosity.

The shelves had been removed and there were small canvases stacked inside. They were some of his unsold paintings, I realized. A wave of pity washed over me. He didn't need to hide his paintings, I thought, we could hang them in the house. The world may not have recognized him as a great painter, but I still believed in him. Gautam's safe was open. It was empty, except for something lying at the back. An iPhone. I smiled. Gautam must have sold a painting. I was glad he had been able to buy a new one. I picked up the phone.

It was dead, and I knew why. I recognized it. It was my iPhone.

Everything came back to me in a rush—the chain snatching, the abrasion on my neck, my inability to sleep on either side because of the injury, the loss of my gold chain and the iPhone Gautam was unable to sell, because I had mentioned the IMEI number in the FIR I had lodged with the police. Gautam entered the room. He saw the Godrej almirah wide open and the iPhone in my hand. His face turned ashen.

'Why did you do it?' I asked Gautam. 'Why did you stage the chain snatching?'

'You said a servant did it. What am I but a glorified servant in this house? You treat me like one. I have to beg you for money. You have so much of it while I have none,' he said, suddenly full of passionate anger. He was a wimp, I thought.

'Who was the chain snatcher?' I asked.

'Someone who owed me a favour,' Gautam said sullenly.

'What did you do with the money?' I knew that the chain would have fetched him about two lakh rupees, or more.

'I spent it,' he muttered.

'Did you tell him to hurt me?' I persisted.

'Just a little,' Gautam said, a little embarrassed, 'for the years of humiliation I suffered.' That was when I lost it. I picked up the golf club lying near the bed and brought it down on his head. I heard a sickening crunch as he crumpled and fell on to the floor.

The Iconoclast

The silence outside the hospital room was deafening. The students who had been shouting raucously a few days ago, exhorting the government to accede to their demands, were bereft. Their beloved teacher, lying amidst a tangle of tubes, was being readied for an emergency bypass. His condition was critical and he was hovering between life and death.

'Sir is our guru,' Sumit said, dabbing at his eyes. 'If anything happens to him …'

'Shh,' said Rachit, 'don't say anything. Be positive. Let us pray that his surgery is successful.'

'How will we organize the rally tomorrow without him?' Amit asked. 'He's the only one at the university who was supporting us.'

The students recalled Abhijit Banerjee standing on the podium, his voice stentorian and his head thrown back, his crisp pyjama kurta hanging loosely around his lanky frame as he described the atrocities on the Dalits throughout the centuries, reminding people of the time when Dalit men and women were not allowed to cast their shadow on the street when a Brahmin walked by. He spoke of Dr Bhim Rao Ambedkar's humiliation as a student, when his teacher refused to allow him to enter the classroom. He spoke of the plight of Karan, the 'sutputra' in the Mahabharata. He spoke of a fractured and divided society, which had subjugated and humiliated Dalits for centuries.

'We owe them reservations at the least,' he said, 'in perpetuity.'

The university hall resounded with applause whenever he spoke. Abhijit Banerjee could draw crowds and hold them spellbound with his oration.

'Had Sir been there, Soumitra would never have committed suicide,' Amit said sadly, recalling his friend's suicide a few days ago when Dr Abhijit Banerjee had been out of town. 'If only Sir had not been away at that time. He was the voice of sanity. The voice of reason.'

The Dalit students had started an agitation when the government had proposed restricting the reservations for the scheduled caste and scheduled tribe, only to the first-generation beneficiaries. Nothing was likely to come of it, but the Dalit students and Dalit sympathizers wanted to pre-empt any such move. The university had tried to quell the agitation. Abhijit Banerjee had advised the students to use the Gandhian tactics of satyagraha and ahimsa.

'Fast unto death,' he had said, 'and I shall join you.'

Of course, the students had known that Abhijit Banerjee's participation would only be symbolic. He was an insulin-dependent diabetic and diabetics cannot go on indefinite hunger strikes, otherwise their blood sugar levels plummet. No one wanted him to go into hypoglycemic shock.

'We will begin the operation in an hour,' said the doctor, 'but we require four bottles of blood in stock.'

Mrs Suruchi Banerjee, his wife, looked distressed. She was

underweight, as was her daughter Shweta, but she needn't have worried. The whole university was willing to donate blood for Dr Banerjee.

'Just three days ago he was closeted with the Vice Chancellor,' Amit disclosed, 'vehemently opposing the action the students who had held demonstrations within their colleges. He had argued that the Vice Chancellor could not have them arrested for exercising their freedom of speech and expression which was their constitutional right. I remember him telling me about it.'

Shweta's eyes were red from weeping.

'It must've been something you said,' she told her mother, her tone bitter.

'Why?' bristled Suruchi. 'You must have. You are bound by tradition. "Don't eat meat, don't enter the kitchen in your footwear, don't ...." Shweta mimicked her mother. 'You must have said something to him to cause the heart attack.'

Her mother's face began to flush.

'I said nothing,' she said, her mouth grim.

'Really?' Shweta said furiously. 'The servants said that you were closeted with Papa for half an hour, after which you rushed out and called an ambulance. You must have said something which caused his heart attack.'

Suruchi opened her mouth to say something, then clamped it shut. Shweta looked at her triumphantly. She knew she was right.

Suruchi recalled the day Shweta had come home, arm in arm with Sumit.

'Mummy,' Shweta said, 'Sumit has just proposed to me.'

Suruchi had simply said 'Congratulations'. She liked Sumit. He was a regular visitor at their house. He was a PhD scholar with good prospects of teaching at a university. If he wrote the civil service examination, she was certain that he would qualify.

'Where is Papa?' Shweta had asked.

'He has not returned from the university,' she had informed them.

Her husband had only returned hours later. He had slumped into a chair, pulled off his socks and thrown them towards his wife. Suruchi had picked them up and kept them away, wondering why he couldn't do it himself.

'It was a very satisfying meeting,' he said, 'the Vice Chancellor listened to everything I said.'

'I have some news for you,' she interrupted excitedly.

'How many times have I told you not to interrupt me when I'm speaking?' he rasped.

She fell silent. Anything for a bit of peace and quiet. It had taken her years to practise restraint; by now she was good at it. His monologue ended half an hour later. Then she said, 'Sumit has asked Shweta to marry him.'

'Who?' he said.

'Sumit Das,' she responded.

'Sumit Das and Shweta. Our Shweta?' he asked, his eyes bulging. 'Impossible.'

'Why?' she asked, alarmed.

'We are Kulin Brahmins, while he,' Abhijit Banerjee spat out the word, 'is a Dalit.'

'But you are the biggest advocate of Dalits in the university,' she said, aghast.

'I may be, but no daughter of mine can marry one. I will not allow it.'

'I think Shweta might say yes,' Suruchi said. She saw his

face turn red, and then mottled. He clutched his heart and then fell down. Sweat poured down his face, leaving Suruchi in no doubt about the fact that he was having a heart attack.

'What triggered the heart attack?' the cardiologist asked Suruchi.

'This whole agitation, and the rustication of the students being contemplated by the university, well, he took it all to heart,' she said in a pensive tone, unwilling to admit that her husband, the biggest votary of Dalits, had feet of clay.

'Please ensure that he is given no distressing news. It may trigger another heart attack,' cautioned the cardiologist.

Five days later, Abhijit Banerjee was wheeled out of the ICU into a private room. Suruchi had just stepped outside to purchase medicines when she saw Shweta and Sumit rushing towards Abhijit Banerjee's room.

'Wait, just wait,' Suruchi shouted. The cardiologist, who came walking past, looked at them indulgently.

'I allowed them to go. Sumit wanted to give him the news personally that Shweta had accepted his proposal. Henceforth, he would not just be Abhijit Banerjee's favourite student, but also his son-in-law.'

Suruchi slumped on a nearby bench. She was certain that the second heart attack would come soon. She wondered who Shweta would blame this time.